CHICK FLICK

ALOHA CHICKEN MYSTERIES: BOOK 10

Josi Avari

Quill
Canyon
Press

Want to know about new releases, free books, and
fabulous prizes? Sign up for my newsletter!
josiavari.com
and connect with me on facebook

Chick Flick

First edition. September 24, 2020.

Copyright © 2020 Josi Avari.

Written by Josi Avari.

Cover art and illustrations by Richard Lance Russell

See more at richardrussellart.com

Chapter One

"Roll sound, roll camera!"

Tangible energy coursed through the group, as real as the wind that set the palm trees around them gently swaying. Saffron tried to remember exactly where she was supposed to walk, where she was supposed to stop. They had shot this scene three times, and still the director wasn't satisfied.

"Back in line!" hissed Holly Oliver. Holly was Saffron's new friend. She had talked Saffron into spending her Thursday on the set of the movie filming in Maika'i, the little Hawaiian town where Saffron ran Hau'oli ka Moa Egg Farm and Bright-blossom Events.

Holly's exclamation made Saffron giggle. The Production Assistant in charge of shepherding them around the set, however, found it much less amusing. She scowled at them and shook her head.

Saffron figured she was annoyed partly because the scene was beginning and partly because it was her words that Holly was parroting. The PA had been bossing them around since they arrived this morning, which, Saffron realized, was her job. She smiled back at the PA to show she understood.

The director, Elias Blum, was a taskmaster, and Saffron was sure the PA was just trying to keep from getting yelled at . . . again. Blum had given the whole cast and crew a lecture this morning about exactly how much each second was costing, and warned them that if they held up production or messed up shots, they would be personally responsible for wasting the studio's dollars.

Blum was a thin man, angular and driven. Saffron had seen him in his director's chair twice now, as the PA shuttled them from place to place on the set, and she'd never seen anyone sit like Blum did. It was as if he were a vine and his director's chair the arbor. As he sat peering at the set, he twisted himself around the chair in every way he possibly could: his legs were entangled with the legs of the chair, his feet twisted around as if he were clinging to it in a hurricane. Each arm wove its way around the back or under the arm of the chair. His hands slipped between the canvas seat and the wooden frame. He was completely wrapped around it. The contorted posture in which he directed, his booming voice, and his sharp eyes all combined to make Saffron very unwilling to cross him, too. She could see why he made the PA nervous.

Holly didn't seem nervous. She seemed to be having the time of her life. Saffron was glad she was here, and glad they'd become friends. Holly owned the Sprout Shop, Maika'i's new plant nursery and floral design business. They had met just three weeks ago, when Saffron had seen a stunning flower arrangement at the Laki Luau. She'd discovered that it was the work of the new florist, and she'd been eager to meet the artist who had created it. She'd gone to the Sprout Shop and ended up hiring Holly to do the flowers for a wedding she was coordinating.

"Action!" Saffron leaned around to catch a glimpse of the two principal actors. Like everyone else in the crowd of extras, she'd shown up this morning hoping for a glance at Zayne Grayson, the male lead.

Instead, she'd mostly spent the day looking at the stringy hair on the back of the head of a guy named Rob, the extra who happened to be in front of her in the crowd scene they were shooting. Rob was nice enough, but he was no Zayne Grayson.

Saffron wasn't sure if it was Zayne himself that put butterflies in her stomach, or the roles he had recently played. Zayne was the star of three recent romantic comedies, each more heart-warming than the last. The film they were shooting today would be the fourth.

Saffron heard their cue and started walking, trying to look as if she hadn't walked this stretch of beach sixteen times since breakfast. She was one of the "random tourists" that populated the beach while Zayne and his love interest, played by Elyse Avery, had an argument. Saffron didn't know what the argument was about, or what the central conflict of the movie was. She just knew that part of it happened here on the beach.

Though they hadn't provided Saffron with any information beyond the idea that she was a typical tourist, she had made up, in her mind, a character to play. She imagined herself as Gwen Thistledown, a schoolteacher from Minnesota whose life was passing her by. Upon realizing she'd never seen the ocean, Gwen had decided to take a vacation to Hawaii.

Saffron painted a look of wonder across her face as she took in the azure ocean, the pristine sky, the whitecaps, and a sea turtle riding the surf. It didn't even feel like acting, because that awe still lived in Saffron. She'd moved here from the drab streets of Washington, DC, and she still thrilled at the island's rich colors, its fragrant breezes, and its sweet ocean music.

Gwen would be overwhelmed right now, Saffron thought, at the difference between Minnesota and Hawaii. She pulled out her phone and snapped a photo as she walked to send to Gwen's bridge club back home. She tried to move like Gwen— a little more gingerly than she moved in her own actual life. She struggled to walk across the beach because Gwen had never fought the shifting sand before. She was so caught up in her character that when she felt sand in her shoe, she paused briefly and stood on one foot, slipping it off and shaking it out as she gazed at the ocean.

"Cut, cut, cut!" Elias Blum bellowed.

Saffron looked up to see Holly gesturing wildly from off-camera, waving to Saffron to catch up. It was then that Saffron noticed that her group of extras had gone on without her. She stood alone on the beach behind Zayne Grayson and Elyse Avery, with the whole production crew staring at her.

Saffron didn't bother to put her shoe back on. She scooted across the beach to huddle beside Holly, her breath coming fast with embarrassment.

She hoped they'd reset the scene—expected them to. Instead, the director disentangled himself from his chair and stood, his wiry frame unbending to its full height. He reached out a hand and someone handed him a bullhorn.

"Get those extras over here!" he said, "all of them!"

Several people, including Rob, cast angry looks at Saffron and murmured, "Way to go!" or "Now we're all in trouble."

The PA got them trotting toward Blum by shouting, "Come on, then, let's go!" and then looping around to the back of the group like a cowdog. Saffron thought that if she looked back, she might see the PA nipping at the heels of any straggling extras.

Blum eyed them as they arrived. Saffron huddled in the middle of the group. Holly took her hand and gave her an encouraging look. Saffron smiled back weakly.

"Do you all remember how much each second of a production day costs?" Blum barked, tossing the bullhorn to a nearby assistant. He certainly had enough volume without it.

The extras mumbled that they did.

"Then why, do you think, we've had to shoot this scene over and over and over? Do you honestly believe that Mr. Grayson over there and Ms. Avery are holding us up?" Blum eyed the extras, and they shook their heads obediently. "No. That's right. They are consummate professionals. Probably able to polish this scene off in a single take. The lighting and camera crews are doing their jobs. Everyone is out here doing their best work, yet we keep having to reshoot. Does anyone know why that is?"

Saffron had just met most of these extras today, so she shouldn't have expected much loyalty from them. Still, she was surprised when they united in throwing her directly under the bus.

"It's her!" there was pointing, "She's not paying attention!"

"She's walking too slow!"

"I saw her take a picture!" this was from Rob.

"Et tu, Rob?" Saffron gave him a disappointed look.

"You. Redhead. Come here, please," Blum shouted. Saffron felt her cheeks burning as the extras parted and she walked to the front. Holly waved a little goodbye as she let go of Saffron's hand.

"Who are you?" Blum asked.

"Saffron Skye, Sir."

"I don't care about your name. Who are you in this scene?"

"Oh!" heart pounding from humiliation, Saffron launched into her story before she could think, "Gwen Thistledown, from Minnesota. I teach third grade. I've never seen the ocean, so I decided to come to Hawaii before my life passed me by completely." Saffron realized how ridiculous it all sounded when she said it out loud in front of all these people.

Blum's face was inscrutable, "And did you stop to take a photo during that shot?"

Saffron's voice squeaked with fear. She reminded herself that it didn't matter if she got fired. She was only getting paid $75 for the day anyway, "Yes."

"Why?"

"To—to send to Gwen's bridge club back home."

"Imaginary Gwen's imaginary bridge club?" he said, his voice acidic.

"Mm-hmm," was all Saffron could manage.

Blum shifted his gaze to the other extras. He pointed a long finger at Rob, "You!" he said.

Rob stood up straight, his stringy hair stirring in the breeze, "Yes, Mr. Blum?"

"Who are you in this scene?"

Rob knew the answer. The right answer. The answer they'd been told from the beginning of the day, the answer that was on the paperwork they'd filled out this morning. They'd each been instructed to write the same thing under the heading where it said "Role."

"A tourist," Rob piped up.

Blum pointed at another extra, "And you? Who are you in this scene?"

"A tourist," he repeated.

"And you?" Blum pointed at Holly, who shot an apologetic expression at Saffron as she answered, "A tourist."

Blum turned back to Saffron, "They're all tourists, and you're Gwen Thistledown from Minnesota," he said.

Saffron nodded.

The tirade he then unleashed could have, Saffron thought, won him an award for Most Angry Director, if there had been such an award.

"That, everyone, is why we've had to reshoot this scene ad infinitum this morning. That is why poor Mr. Grayson and poor Ms. Avery have had to say their lines over and over and over. That is why this movie, from a major production company, with an enormous budget, still looks like something shot with a family video camera in the local city park. Because YOU," here, to Saffron's surprise, he pointed that long, accusing finger at the crowd of extras, not at her, "refuse to invest in it."

There were surprised exclamations through the crowd.

"I have a beach full of bad actors whose only thoughts are either to get from point 'a' to point 'b' or to saunter close enough to the camera to get into the shot. This woman is the only—I repeat, the only—one of you that remembers the reason we're actually here: to tell a story. She looks natural, she knows her character. She sets the scene instead of trying to steal it. You're not hear to be 'a tourist.' You're here to make this scene feel like a real beach on an ordinary day. You have one more try, and if you can't pull this off, I'm cutting you all from the scene."

The indignant extras had quieted. Blum waved a hand, "Get them back to starting positions," he told the PA. "Let's try again and see if they can possibly manage to act like they're not acting."

The PA rounded them up again, and Saffron began to move away with the group.

"Wait," Blum called, and they all paused, looking back over their shoulders at him, "You, Gwen Thistledown, clear your schedule. I want you on set tomorrow. I've got a speaking part for you."

Chapter Two

A soft rain had sprinkled the egg farm when Saffron arrived home late that afternoon. The sun, pushing the clouds away, worked to steam the moisture off the foliage and fill the air with the drops that had just fallen. Saffron breathed in the island perfume: rain and salt, rich earth and light, sweet plumeria.

The light changed quickly as Saffron made her way down to the egg house to check on the hens.

She passed the three bungalows that sat on the other side of her driveway. The cottages were painted in bright colors: banana yellow, coral pink, and the brilliant teal of a Pacific lagoon.

Saffron had renovated these cottages after she moved to the egg farm, and they gave her quite a nice income in addition to the eggs she sold and the events she planned.

Sometimes vacation rentals were inconvenient, and some of her renters over the years had been less than pleasant, but she enjoyed meeting new people, and she liked having some neighbors, even if they were just temporary ones.

The cottages were empty just now, awaiting a group that

should arrive any moment. Saffron was glad they were coming today. Though she had installed door handles with a code so guests could check themselves in, she did like to greet them. She might not be able to do that if they came tomorrow, since she had no idea how long she'd be on the set.

A speaking part. She thought of that as she trailed her fingers along the bushes, glistening with raindrops. She'd never had a burning desire to be an actress, so she'd never thought of how she would present herself on camera until today. But the director's praise and her successful performance as an extra had sparked something in her.

It had been freeing to become Gwen Thistledown. Saffron liked stepping into that other life and pretending for a moment that she was someone else. The thought of who she'd be tomorrow stirred a little swirl of excitement in her stomach.

The hens were chatting to each other as Saffron approached. Their pens inside the egg house were attached to spacious outdoor runs by little doors. About half the hens were inside, staying dry, while the other half were outside in the long, damp grass searching for bugs upset by the rain.

Tikka, Saffron's beautiful black and gold hen, chortled a hello as she approached. Saffron was munching on a croissant filled with guava cream from the catering tables back at the movie set. Though she was enjoying it thoroughly, she knew that Tikka would go crazy for it, so she tore off a bit and tossed it to the hen through the wire of the outdoor run.

Tikka snatched it, frantically trying to eat it before her flockmates, Cleo, Luna, and Blossom, noticed she had it.

She was too late. Cleo, a heavy-breed chicken called a Buff Brahma, rushed over and used her bulk to slam sideways into Tikka. The bit of bread flew from her beak, sparking the interest of Luna and Blossom. The two fluffy hens made a waddling run in the direction of the croissant.

But Tikka didn't give up that easily. She ran, too, her soft bustle of underfeathers bouncing as she caught up to Cleo.

Blossom, a bit lighter breed than the other three hens, reached the croissant first and tore off a beakful just as Luna and Cleo snatched it away, tearing it into two pieces. Blossom gobbled her bite and gave a happy chirp.

Tikka headed for Cleo and the two hens grappled over the last bit, eventually tearing it down the middle. Each ran to a separate corner to enjoy her prize.

Saffron found herself smiling, "Nothing like a good game of chicken football, eh, girls?" To Saffron, the hens' competition to grab any treat looked just like a game of football—everyone focused on a single prize and willing to knock anyone down who got between them and their goal.

Inside the egg house, the dry hens were scratching at the sand of their pens and pecking at their feeders. Saffron turned the crank on the mechanical feeding system that sent more pellets of food rattling to each pen. She checked the automatic watering system and cranked the conveyor that brought the afternoon's crop of eggs down to the work area where she stood.

Muddy days were more work for Saffron—she had to run the eggs through the washing system in the work area. But placing them in their cartons an hour later, washed and polished to a glowing sheen, Saffron felt the surge of pride and accomplishment that made egg farming so satisfying.

She was just placing the last of the eggs in their cartons when she heard a loud braying from the corral across the farmyard and a popping cluck from just outside the egg house door. The first sound was an alarm from Jasper, Saffron's donkey. The second, a warning call from Saffron's free-roaming porch rooster, Curry. Both wanted Saffron to be aware that there was something out of the ordinary happening on the farm.

The guests must be arriving. Saffron closed the final carton and went to greet them.

She was expecting the usual tourists: some pasty Midwestern software engineer and his siblings and their spouses, usually with a few kids in tow. She made a note to set out the new boogie boards she'd bought this week for the new arrivals.

But these were not her usual guests. As Saffron approached the blue rental car parked in front of the Coral Cottage, a man turned toward her whose broad shoulders, chiseled jaw, and pale grey eyes could only belong to one person.

"Zayne Grayson?" Saffron's voice was high and thready with surprise.

As the passenger from the car climbed out, Saffron gasped a little, "and Elyse Avery?"

The back door opened and a small man hopped out and spread his arms, looking Saffron in the eye with his eyebrows raised. He clearly expected her to gasp his name, too.

Saffron wrinkled her brow in concentration. She had seen him before. She knew he was an actor. What had he been in?

He was waiting expectantly for her recognition. "You're the guy in that show . . ." she began, ". . . about the submarine . . . The one that got bit by the shark, but survived?" she said hopefully.

He dropped his arms and bunched his face into an expression of disgruntled acceptance, "Ace—" he began.

"Carnation!" Saffron finished with him, "Ace Carnation!"

He smiled good-naturedly, "You were half right."

Elyse leaned on the car, smiling indulgently, while Zayne gazed at the cottages.

"Are you lost?" Saffron asked, "I can give you directions back to your hotel." Everyone in Maika'i knew, everyone in the world knew, that they were staying at the Little Hawaii Resort, in their most luxurious suites.

Zayne's warm smile sparkled—the one that FlashStar Magazine called "the smile that launched a thousand sighs." He gestured toward the cottages, "Actually," he said, "We're staying here."

"But the news said—"

"It's a little switcheroo," Ace popped in, "See, if we stay there, we've got paparazzi camped outside our rooms, shooting photos of us at the pool, documenting our failed attempts to pick up ladies . . ." Ace winked.

Zayne's deep voice chimed in, "but if we tell them we're staying there, then leave and stay at a quaint little out of the way vacation rental instead, we have a lot more privacy."

"And a lot more fun," Ace finished for him.

"You're—you're my renters?" Saffron couldn't remember the name on the reservation, but she was certain it wasn't Zayne Grayson. She would have remembered that.

They smiled indulgently. This was not a new situation to them. Saffron pulled her thoughts together and pushed aside her excitement. They were her renters, and she needed to be professional.

"Please," she said, waving a hand at the cottages, "this way."

She led them to the Coral Cottage, and gave them a quick tour. They were gracious and enthusiastic. It was strange to see them not made up, not in movie wardrobe. They joked with each other, and were all-around very personable.

They would each be staying in one of the three cottages: Ace in the Banana cottage, Zayne in the Pacific Lagoon Cottage, and Elyse in the Coral Cottage. Saffron showed them where the spare towels were, pointed them to the beach, and left them in peace. After all, that's what they had come for.

THEY HAD ASKED Saffron to keep it quiet that they were staying there, and she tried. She honestly tried. When Nik, her boyfriend, came that night for dinner, she didn't blurt out the secret like she was dying to do.

She was fixing a local favorite: loco moco. When she'd first arrived, she'd secretly thought it looked like a meal made out of random parts of other meals: rice, a fried egg, a hamburger patty, and gravy. But despite its strange appearance, it was delicious and the perfect end to a long and surprising day.

Tonight she was making a variation she'd learned from her friend Bernadette at the Oceanside Cafe, her favorite eatery in Maika'i. For this version of loco moco, she'd added sweet, tangy Hawaiian barbecue sauce to the ground beef and crunchy bamboo shoots to the fried egg. She'd topped it with a garlicky ranch gravy and sprinkled crispy fried onions over the top.

When plated up, it wasn't quite as photogenic as the one Bernadette served, but it tasted just as good.

Nik was a classic surfer: blond and tanned, always slouching and always smiling. He took very little in life seriously. It was a nice balance to her more intense and careful personality.

"I think I have a good shot," he said. Lately, he was totally obsessed with a surfing competition coming up. Nik was working at becoming a professional surfer, and Saffron was excited to see how far he could go—she'd never seen anyone so talented on a board. "How was your day on the set?" he asked excitedly, taking a bite of rice, "did you see anyone famous?"

Saffron shoveled a big forkful into her mouth to keep from answering. She just nodded.

"Did you see Zayne Grayson? Somebody said they saw him in a limo on Holoholo Street!"

Saffron nodded again, still chewing.

"And Elyse Avery bought something at Fumi's kitchen

store!" he said this like it was the most amazing thing that had ever happened. Saffron raised her eyebrows and nodded.

"Did you see her on set?"

"Mmm-hmmm."

"I wouldn't mind seeing her," Nik said, grinning. "She's a knockout. And you know, she always looks good, no matter what. There's never any photos of her in the tabloids with big dark circles under her eyes or her hair all messed up. I don't know how she stays looking so perfect all the time."

Saffron fixed him with a harsh gaze and it only took him one blink to realize that Saffron was not interested in hearing his glowing report of Elyse Avery's looks.

Nik backtracked, "I mean, it's probably all that plastic surgery." He smiled sheepishly and Saffron gave him a doubtful, but forgiving, look.

"Well, if its movie stars you're into," she said, "you'll be happy to know that I have to go back tomorrow because the director wants me to do a speaking part."

"What? No way! Sweet!" Nik grilled her for the next few minutes for details, most of which she didn't yet have.

She was describing the amazing catering when Nik's eyes, gazing out the window past her, got huge. Saffron realized that though Nik loved good food, it was not her description of the lilikoi cake and the shrimp canapes that were amazing him. She turned and saw, walking down the driveway toward the beach, Elyse Avery.

"Is that—" he started.

"I didn't tell you," she said, letting out a huge breath of relief.

"Didn't tell me what?"

"I wasn't supposed to say anything."

"Wait, is she staying in your cottage?"

Saffron nodded, "But I didn't tell you—you saw them for yourself."

"Them?"

Saffron pressed her lips together. Though her father had worked for the FBI, she was no good at intrigue herself.

"He's here, too? Zayne?"

Saffron nodded.

"Wow!" Nik jumped up and went to the window, peering toward the cottages. Saffron went over and saw her other two renters on the porch of the banana cottage. "And that guy!" he said, "The plucky comic relief!"

THE MOON HAD RISEN on the water, turning the sea into a bright mirror. Saffron walked along the sand, her hand in Nik's. They were discussing the surfing competition.

"I think I'll do okay, but it's hard to know for sure," he said, "the resort in Dayton has the most advanced artificial wave pool in the world, but I just don't know how much like the actual ocean it's going to be."

"What do the other surfers say?" Saffron asked, glancing up at his profile in the moonlight.

"They say it's the world's most perfect wave," the timbre of Nik's voice shifted to that warm tone he used when he talked about surfing, "that it's a perfect barrel at the flip of a switch. It's longer than any natural wave, so you can really show off your best moves to the judges."

"Well, then, they're going to be blown away, because you've got some great moves to show off."

Nik chuckled and stopped on the sand. He slipped his free hand around Saffron's waist, turning to face her, "You like my moves, huh?"

Saffron felt the butterflies Nik always set off in her stomach. She met him halfway as he leaned in for a kiss.

"I'm going to miss you while I'm on the road," he said. "Miss this."

The purring of the waves beside them and the warmth of the night around them reminded Saffron how Hawaii got into your soul, "Even if it makes great waves, I don't think Dayton will have the power of the islands," Saffron agreed.

"Or the beauty of the islands," Nik's teeth flashed white in the darkness and Saffron's face flushed.

"Will you come watch me? In one of the competitions?"

"Of course," Saffron said, "I wouldn't miss it."

"Listen, Saffron, I know we've had some, you know, tough times. With the fall and everything," Saffron shifted as a pang of memory shot through her, "but you're really . . . Important to me, and I totally . . ." Nik swallowed, "like you."

Nik didn't express himself often. He'd lost his parents early in life, and Saffron assumed that emotional vulnerability was just harder for him than for other people. He shied away from serious conversations, especially about their relationship. But here, on the quiet beach, she heard everything he was saying and not saying.

He was worried about the time they'd be apart. He was feeling apprehensive about the competition. He knew he was going to be homesick. Nik spent his days in the surf shop or on the water, with no cares and no drama beyond the disappointment of missing a great curl or having a spectacular wipeout. He wasn't used to emotion.

Saffron reached up and laid a hand on his cheek, catching his gaze in the dark. "It's going to be okay, Nik. You're going to crush the competition and rock the surfing world." She knew how to speak his language.

He kissed her again.

"That's a wrap," a jovial voice from the shadow of a nearby palm tree made the two leap apart. Onto the moon-swept beach walked Saffron's third guest—not Zayne, not Elyse, the other guy.

Saffron shot him a scowl but wasn't sure he saw it clearly.

"No, really," he said, a New York City accent hovering behind his words, "that was a perfect romantic scene."

"Dude!" Nik called. It was a word he used for many meanings, so Saffron waited, out of habit, for the follow-up before deciding if he was scolding the man for interrupting them or exclaiming in excitement.

It was the latter, "I can't believe you're actually here in town! I loved you in that one movie where you were, like, the guy's best friend."

Dryly, the man responded, "That's pretty much every movie I've *ever* been in."

Nik laughed, "Seriously, though, you're great!"

"Well, thanks, Dude," the man echoed Nik, "now if only you remembered my name." There was an air of light sarcasm in his voice, but Saffron couldn't tell if it was intentional or just a product of his accent.

"Naw, dude, I remember your name. It's—" if Nik hadn't gone so confidently into the first half of the sentence, the second half wouldn't have been so awkward, ". . . Al . . . Bill . . . Chuck?"

"Are you going to go through the whole alphabet?" the man quipped. Saffron wanted to help Nik, but the man's name had escaped her, too. Nik stopped guessing, and there was a long, painful moment where the only sound was the waves.

"Ace," the man offered.

"Right! Ace Carnation!" Nik was truly delighted to be meeting a star.

"Now you got it."

"You've been all over the papers!" Nik said, "For that brawl at the Walk of Fame. I heard you bled on John Wayne's star."

"If anybody should understand getting a little roughed up in a fistfight," Ace said dryly, "it should be the Duke."

"Maybe I shouldn't say anything about all the gossip," Nik's tone was apologetic.

Ace waved him off, "Aw, kid, in Hollywood *any* press is good press. I'm a lot more afraid of being forgotten than I am of being remembered badly."

Saffron was not interested in Ace's antics. She was still feeling a little intruded upon, "Just out for a midnight stroll, Mr. Carnation?"

"Kid, nobody calls me Mr. Carnation. Even my secretary calls me Ace," he jerked his head, indicating the long stretch of silvery beach, "Yeah, just taking a walk. I'm a bit of an insomniac. This place is nice and quiet."

"Wait until morning," Saffron said, "you'll probably hear my rooster, Curry."

"Can't be any worse than the parrot they've got on set," Ace growled.

"There's a parrot?"

"Oh, yeah, it's Elyse's character's pet in the script, but they have to put it in the makeup trailer whenever it's not in the scene because it's so loud and obnoxious."

Saffron and Nik looked at each other, "Echo?" they asked together.

"That's right. You know that crazy bird?"

"Yeah, Echo's a local," Saffron shrugged, "she belongs to the owner of our pet shop here in town."

"Well, she's certainly got opinions."

"She's also a little kleptomaniacal, so watch your valuables," Saffron warned.

Ace laughed, the sound passing Saffron by and continuing off across the waves in the darkness, "Well, she must have been typecast then. That's exactly what she does in the film."

"What? Steal stuff?"

"Yeah, at least in the big meet-cute scene she does."

"Meet-cute scene?"

"Sure, you know, there's one in every romantic comedy? Where the main guy and the main girl meet in some cute way? Like they reach for the same pair of gloves in the department store on Christmas Eve? Or he comes to the dock and asks to rent her father's fishing boat for a week?"

"Okay," Saffron admitted, "I know the scene you mean."

"Well in this movie, the meet-cute happens when Elyse's character's parrot flies over and grabs Zayne's sunglasses off his head. She's chasing the bird, and he's chasing his sunglasses, and when they meet the sparks fly. It's that moment that they see each other and their eyes get all starry and the audience starts hoping they'll get together."

"Huh, I never knew there was a name for that moment," Saffron mused.

"Oh, kid, every moment in Hollywood has a name."

Chapter Three

The romance had not returned after Ace Carnation's interruption. Nik had spent the rest of the evening raving about how cool it was that Saffron got to spend time on set and be in an actual movie.

When she walked into the Oceanside Cafe with her arms full of egg cartons the next morning, she'd had lots of practice dealing with an adoring fan. It was a good thing, too, because her father, Slate Skye, and her adopted grandpa and dear friend, Mano Kekoa, were having breakfast at the cafe.

"We heard you're a star!" Slate wrapped her in a bear hug.

"Easy," she said into his shoulder, "the eggs!"

"Oh, sorry," he loosened his grip and took several cartons from her, "but I'm just pretty proud of my daughter the actress!"

Mano stood and greeted her. She pressed her forehead to his, inhaling deeply. It was a greeting that he had always shared with her—the honi—and it symbolized the sharing of their life force. It always made Saffron feel seen and valued and present in that moment.

Mano smiled and took more egg cartons from her arms.

Together, the three carried the eggs into the kitchen, where Bernadette exclaimed over Saffron's part in the movie, too.

Saffron was glad to slip back into the booth with Mano and Slate for a few minutes to steal some nibbles of their breakfasts. Slate was having mango French toast, and Mano was indulging in the macadamia nut chocolate cake. Together, the two made a rich, tart combination. Saffron thought she should propose chocolate mango macadamia nut french toast to Bernadette.

"Where are you filming today?" Mano asked conversationally, offering her a forkful of cake.

Saffron took it and said, "Shell Beach." It was the broad stretch of golden sand just north of town. It had a lovely event center nestled in a grove of hala trees that shielded it from the road.

"Oh, that'll be a nice place to spend the day," Mano nodded. Something about his tone made Saffron peer at him. Mano was never sarcastic, so what was that strange inflection in his voice?

She didn't have time to ask. Glancing at her watch, she realized she needed to get the next egg delivery down the road to the Paradise Market and then get over for hair and makeup. She grabbed one last bite of her dad's French Toast, popped a kiss on the top of each man's head, and rushed out.

The Paradise Market was bustling this morning, and Saffron was glad to get their eggs delivered.

It was a bright, open market with a yellow and green color scheme. The shelves were always well-stocked, and the whole place smelled of fresh pineapple and baking bread.

Saffron headed to the egg cooler, where she always made her deliveries. She stopped in at the office in the back to tell her friends, the owners of the market, Baruti and Tale, that she'd left the eggs. As soon as Saffron popped her head in the door, Baruti turned from the filing cabinet he was standing beside. He stepped forward and greeted Saffron with the the traditional handshake he'd brought from Botswana: a clasp, a twist, then he placed his left hand under his right elbow. Saffron did the same. Again, the greeting took focus, concentration. It was an intimate acknowledgement of their friendship.

It occurred to Saffron how important it was to stop and take a moment to truly see someone else, to look into their eyes and strengthen the bond. She had learned so many new ways of greeting while living in Hawaii, so many new ways of truly seeing others.

"Ahhhh," Baruti said, "I knew I should have rolled out the red carpet this morning."

"Oh, stop. It's a tiny part," Saffron waved him off.

"No small parts," Tale scolded, throwing a wave to Saffron. She was seated in front of the computer, making out next week's orders, "This I had to tell Baruti time and again."

Saffron raised her eyebrows, "Baruti! You're an actor?"

"I was," he said modestly. He was tall and angular, with a tight flat-top and a brilliant smile. Saffron could see that he would be a striking figure onscreen.

"You were not just an actor, you were a superstar!" Tale emphasized, rolling her chair over a bit to reach him and pat his arm with pride.

"Really?" Saffron grinned at him.

"Oh, yes," Tale said, "At a prestigious film festival, he won best actor for his film *Kamoso*."

"I would have liked to see that," Saffron said.

"We have a copy. Perhaps we can watch it sometime?" Tale said.

Baruti scoffed, "Oh, no, you don't want to see that."

"It was a beautiful story!" Tale protested, "The title means *Tomorrow* in Setswana, our first language, and it was about this man waiting for his life to begin—tomorrow. Very moving. And Baruti's performance was funny and touching and incredible." She stood and kissed her husband on the cheek.

"I had no idea. Any advice for someone new to the big screen, Baruti?" Saffron absentmindedly picked up a pencil from the desk and spun it in her fingers as they chatted.

Baruti's thoughtful answer gave Saffron some insight into the depth of his experience as an actor, "I would say, just, as you are portraying someone else, don't forget to be yourself. Find your real emotions, your real reactions, and draw on them. If there is a seed of you in the character, then there is a seed of truth, and that's what audiences respond to—the seeds of truth they see on the screen."

———

THE SEEDS OF TRUTH. The phrase rattled around in Saffron's mind as she hustled through the parking lot of the event center at Shell Beach. One of the people from the access crew minding the lot had directed her where to park and where in the building to go for paperwork. After the paperwork, Saffron had been sent to the hair and makeup trailer.

Long mirrors with counters below them lined one wall and several cupboards and drawers lined the other. Makeup kits sat out on the counters. A large square birdcage sat in the corner, currently empty. Echo the parrot must be with Elyse on set just now.

A woman was speaking, filling the room with a sound like an angry mouse. She wore wildly impractical shoes: leopard-print high heels. Saffron tried not to stare at them.

"How many times? How many times should I have to tell you?"

"I promise, Shar, I *swear*, I put everything back in exactly the places you said, I just—"

"This is the biggest film of my career! I have the opportunity to work with major stars—major stars! I am spending my days on a beach in Hawaii! This is where I belong! I will not go back to working on cow documentaries in Tractorsville, Iowa, just because my assistant is a moron!"

They both looked up at the same time, catching sight of Saffron standing there staring at them.

The man was, in a word, slight. His hair was thin, and his face plain, adorned with circular glasses that looked like they belonged in the eighteen hundreds. They were tinted slightly yellow and they magnified his eyes, giving him the look of a startled gekko.

The woman, Shar, had teased hair that faded from blonde to silver white at the tips. It stuck out like a hedgehog's spikes, making a sharp crown around her pointed face. She had very long false eyelashes. Brushed across her cheeks was a color that Saffron had only seen once before.

Along with Saffron's ability to see more colors than other people came an enormous mental library of colors that allowed her to catalog the colors she'd seen. And because she could see so many colors, she'd had to amass a huge vocabulary of color words to describe them and differentiate between them.

There was no "red" for Saffron. Red was scarlet and garnet and crimson and rose, blood red and rust and overripe raspberry. For some shades she had thousands of references, things she'd seen that matched that exact hue: flowers, fruits, fish. Others occurred much more rarely. The color on Shar's cheeks was one of those.

Saffron was staring, sorting color words in her head until she came to the shade she wanted: it was minium. It was a bright, orangey-red. In the name was her clue to where she'd seen it before, and how she'd learned its proper name. Once, on a trip to Colorado with her mother, she'd picked up a stone with a scaly, crumbling mineral clinging to its sides. She'd learned it was a type of oxidized lead called minium.

The only other place she'd seen it was during a trip to the

Library of Congress, back in Washington, DC. It had been used in some illuminated manuscripts that the curators had been photographing. Saffron still remembered the bright red robes of the figures in the manuscripts. They were just this color.

"Hello?" Shar snapped her fingers in front of Saffron's face, "Character, please?"

"Um," Saffron pulled her focus away from the swaths of minium red on the woman's cheeks and focused on her intense brown eyes, drawing her thoughts together as if scooping seafoam on the tide, "I don't know. Mr. Blum just told me to come back for a speaking part."

Recognition dawned in the woman's eyes, "Oh, okay. That's you. You're the extra that stole the show yesterday. Come on, over here. Roman will look after you."

She gestured to the chair in front of her assistant and Saffron followed her. The door behind them opened, and Saffron glanced back to see another tall man duck into the trailer.

It was as if, suddenly, Saffron did not exist. Shar turned all her attention to the newcomer.

"Adam Sullivan! I cannot wait to get my brushes on you. Oh, Mr. Sullivan! Let me get you ready for this next scene!" Shar ushered him to her chair and began to flit around him like a hummingbird around a flower.

The assistant held out a hand and Saffron sat down, "Do you know who I'm playing?"

Roman referred to some well-worn papers, "Looks like . . . You're the shell-collecting tourist that the principals run into whenever they need sage advice."

"What?"

"Right. You know, a bit part that keeps showing up just when the main characters need to tell the audience something?"

Saffron had never given that much thought to the supporting roles in movies, but now that he mentioned it, Saffron could think of several examples of such characters.

"Okay," he peered closer at the pages, "and it looks like they've written in a name for your character, even though it didn't have one before."

Saffron knew what it would be, "Gwen Thistledown?"

"That's right! How'd you know?"

"She knew," said the handsome man shoulder-to-shoulder with her in the next chair, "because she made it up." Chuckling, he recounted yesterday's events. Saffron watched him in the mirror since Roman had started coating her face with something and she was afraid that if she turned her head at all, she'd lose an eye. Adam Sullivan was charming in that capable, nice-guy way that immediately put Saffron at ease.

"You were on set?"

"Just watching. I had a scene just after that."

"Who do you play?"

He caught her gaze with his brilliant blue eyes, "I play the other man." He winked.

"The other man?"

"You know, the guy that the main girl is with because she can't be with the leading man? The one she tries to convince herself that she loves, even though everyone else, including the audience, can see that she truly loves the leading man and should totally be with him?"

"Oh," Saffron said, "*that* other man."

"Everyone recognizes the character, but nobody remembers him as soon as Zayne Grayson steps onscreen," he didn't seem bothered by that fact.

"Is every character in this movie also in every other romantic comedy?" Saffron asked. It seemed more and more like they were following a pattern here.

"Honey, it's called a trope. Close your eyes," the assistant said, swiping at her eyelids as she did so, "Girl, where in the world did you buy this eyeliner? The grocery store? It is impossible to get off."

Saffron didn't tell him that the Paradise Market was exactly where she had bought her makeup, and that she had chosen it precisely because it stood up to the humid atmosphere and her frequent plunges into the perfect Hawaiian waves.

Roman was scrubbing something on her face that felt like crushed glass.

"Don't you ever exfoliate?" he scolded.

The answer was no. Saffron always figured the sand on her hands when she wiped her face after a great swim was enough to do the trick. Again, she didn't answer Roman.

"Listen," he said, "you're not going to get very far with your speaking part if you can't speak."

"I can," Saffron mumbled as he stood behind her, squashing her cheeks in a circular fashion before stepping away and looking in a cupboard.

"Shar, darling, where are our cleansing wipes?"

"In the cupboard," she snapped, brushing something across Adam Sullivan's forehead.

"They *should* be here," he growled back, "but they are not."

Shar stalked over and ripped the cupbard door out of his hand, grunting in annoyance as she rooted inside.

Saffron, watching them in the mirror, saw Shar give Roman a dangerous look. She could tell the woman wanted to give her assistant a piece of her mind, just as she had been doing when Saffron arrived. Thankfully, Shar restrained herself. Saffron wondered if she should point out that occasionally Echo helped herself to things that weren't hers, but she didn't get a chance. Shar threw the trailer door open and jerked her head for Roman to follow her.

"One moment," she said in Saffron and Adam's general direction, "we'll be right back."

Both make up artists stepped out of the trailer. There was a long, awkward moment of quiet before Adam cleared his throat.

"So, have you always wanted to be an actress?"

"No. It just sort of came up . . . yesterday."

Adam laughed, "Well, a lot of actors would like to get their big break in a major motion picture that easily."

"We'll just see how well I do. I may be fired by lunchtime."

"Hey, with Blum as the director, we may all be fired by lunchtime."

"He does seem pretty intense," Saffron admitted.

"Intensely brilliant. Almost magic."

"Magic? That seems like a pretty strong word for sitting around yelling at people."

Adam shook his head, "Sure, he's tough, but it works. He's directed eight of the ten top-grossing movies of the last decade. He knows, better than anyone, how to tell a story."

Saffron gave him a skeptical look in the mirror, "But from what I'm hearing, he's just telling the same story over and over and over again, right? I mean, the same characters, the same plot points?"

Adam swiveled his chair to face her, and a fine dust flew from his forehead in a little cloud, "Oh, don't get the idea of tropes wrong—sure, they are the same characters and plots, but its how those elements are put together that tell a story. Elias Blum can take our most well-worn patterns and help us see something new—in the story, and in ourselves."

Saffron thought about that. She thought about the Blum movies she'd seen, "You're right. With his films, I never felt like I was watching the same movie again."

"That's the magic," he said with finality.

———————————

SAFFRON LEFT the trailer with a new face and new hair. She was hustled over to wardrobe, where they gave her a big yellow hat, a sundress, and a wrap, along with a bag of seashells and a pair of slippahs.

The Production Assistant from yesterday brought her some pages of the script and introduced her to the character. If Saffron was slightly amused at the woman's strict efficiency yesterday, she was intensely grateful for it today. Saffron had very little time, and a lot to learn. Even the woman's name— Jean Beal—didn't take long to say.

"You'll be on set the rest of the afternoon. Be prepared to do several retakes of the scene. I assume you're okay with being on set for the rest of filming? You have several recurring appearances."

"Yes," Saffron stammered.

"Good. Now. Today, you enter the scene, finding seashells in the background. Adam and Elyse are walking hand in hand searching for shells, but finding nothing remarkable. He notices a shell you've collected and allows her to go on ahead. He then offers to buy it from you for her.

"Your line is, 'Wouldn't it be more romantic if you found it together?' Then he says, 'Don't worry, we will. I'll drop it where she'll be sure to find it.' Then you say, 'It's my best shell. If you want it, it's going to cost you a few clams.' He holds out a wad of cash, you exchange it, then go back to looking for shells. The camera follows him down the beach for the remainder of the scene."

Saffron repeated, "Wouldn't it be more romantic if you found it together? It's my best shell. If you want it, it's going to cost you a few clams." She nodded, "I can remember those."

"Okay. Get into character. They're ready. As you saw yesterday, Blum hates reshooting for supporting roles. He'll do it for principal actors, but he'll flip if you mess up."

"So, no pressure, then?" Saffron tossed a smile at the PA,

but Jean was gone, waving a hand impatiently for Saffron to follow her.

As Saffron stepped out onto the beach, she stepped into Gwen Thistledown's slippahs. Minnesota was far behind her. She had to bring back a shell for her cousin Ann. She loved the warm sand and the way the ocean tickled the tops of her feet. She was Gwen.

She saw what Baruti had meant this morning when he'd said she should find the part of her character that was herself. Though some of Gwen's story was a lie, there was truth in the way Saffron felt about the beach, and in the way she admired the solid little cone shell in her hand.

The next few minutes were a blur as someone showed Saffron where to stand, the camera started rolling, and Adam and Elyse approached. Saffron paid them no attention. She had plenty of practice ignoring other people on the beach, and she drew on that now.

Before she knew it, Adam was approaching. She said her lines, he said his, the shell was exchanged, and her first take was over.

When the AD, or assistant director, yelled "CUT!" Saffron heard a pause, then light clapping. She turned with a growing realization. She knew now why Mano had used that tone earlier.

There, on the edge of the hala grove, sat Mano and Slate in lawn chairs, giving Saffron's performance two thumbs up.

Chapter Four

The men didn't leave when Saffron's scene was over. They sat chatting on the edge of the hala grove, in the shade, drinking cans of their favorite soft drink, POG, which was passion fruit, orange, and guava juice mixed together in a kind of tropical punch.

Saffron didn't blame them—the creation of the film was quality entertainment itself. Assistants rushing here and there, camera operators maneuvering around each other in a complicated dance, lights and sound equipment dipping in from all directions.

And then there were the stars. Elyse and Adam were shooting a walk along the beach where the conflict was introduced into their storyline. Adam would propose and Elyse, instead of crying 'Yes!' and letting him slip the ring on her finger, would hesitate.

The sun had reached its late-morning intensity, and the humidity had climbed. Saffron felt Roman's makeup beginning to soften, and, as she tugged at an itchy eyelid, saw it smudge off on her fingertips. She was glad she didn't have to do this every day.

Elyse, on the other hand, looked as bright and fresh as a flower, even under the constant glare of the hot lights. Of course, it probably helped that Shar darted out every few minutes and powdered, fluffed and sprayed the star.

"I could use someone like that," Saffron said aloud to Jean Beal, who was standing beside her poring over the call sheets, or what Saffron would have called the schedule of the day's events, and the script pages for this scene, some of which were printed on bright yellow paper.

Jean looked up, noted the direction in which Saffron was gazing, then shook her head quickly. "No private touchups for bit parts," she said, "you need a makeup refresher, you go up to the trailer and the assistant will take care of it."

"No, no," Saffron assured her, "I mean in my everyday life. I could use someone to just follow me around and powder and spray me back to perfection anytime a hair got out of place."

Jean squinted at her in confusion and annoyance. Saffron could see that, to the PA, if a conversation didn't have to do with what was happening right now, on set, it wasn't worth having. "Look," she said, "see these yellow pages? Colored pages in a shooting script mean changes. These are changes they made to the script this morning. Just when I had this scene completely down, they've added new lines and blocking, so I have to keep the extras out of the way of these shots. I don't have time to worry about your makeup."

"Sure, sure, I understand. Never mind," Saffron said, giving her an apologetic look.

"Quiet on the set!" yelled the Assistant Director.

Saffron watched with interest as Adam and Elyse walked down the beach in front of the cameras, talking as if they were all alone instead of surrounded by a crew of people recording and analyzing their every step.

"I had no idea you knew how to surf," Elyse was saying.

"I've been sneaking out to take lessons every afternoon," Adam replied, "While you're at your hula class."

"Well, you've picked up some nice moves," Elyse said.

"You like my moves, huh?" Adam's words drew Saffron's focus. That was exactly what Nik had said last night.

As Saffron watched, he slid a hand around Elyse's waist and stepped in front of her, just as Nik had. The two stars kissed.

Saffron looked around to see if anyone else was noticing the eerie similarity to her life that was playing out in front of the camera. Nobody else seemed aware of it.

Saffron tried to convince herself it was a coincidence, but the eerie feeling persisted throughout the rest of the scene.

She pushed it aside as she watched the scene progress.

Elyse played the post-proposal hesitation perfectly, and Adam slipped the velvet ring box with its 2 carat diamond back in his pocket, dejected, as their characters' future together became much less certain. Saffron could see why people enjoyed romantic comedies. In fact, she decided that the predictability she'd been so surprised to recognize before was one of the things people probably liked most about them.

Lunch was anything but predictable. When Saffron approached the long tents set over the loaded tables, she expected the usual crowd food: sandwiches, mac salad, maybe some kalua pork if they were lucky. But this was not usual food. The table was laden with lobster tails, steak, grilled asparagus, salad with capers. And it was a buffet. If Saffron had wanted three lobster tails, she could have gone back and had them.

But there were desserts to try, as well. One whole table was filled with different kinds of cheesecakes. Saffron decided she liked the chocolate mousse one best.

"Hey, you, bit part!" Saffron looked up to see Jean Beal waving her over, holding a take-out box in the air between them.

Saffron approached.

"Listen," the PA said, "I don't usually do this, but Elyse Avery wants cheesecake at the same second that Mr. Blum wants his lunch. Would you be a saint and take her this in her trailer while I take lobster to Blum?"

"Sure," Saffron replied, taking the box.

"I knew you were solid. Thanks!"

The main actors' trailers sat down the beach, making a little village on the sand. Glittering stars on each door helped Saffron navigate.

Just as she set a foot on the metal step, Saffron had to leap backward. The door flew open and a small man bustled out, adjusting his gold-rimmed glasses.

"Excuse me," his voice was rough and higher than Saffron had expected, "my apologies."

"That's okay," Saffron called to his departing back. His hair fell in straight wisps, and as he turned to nod at her, she saw that his chin and jaw were covered with pale rusty stubble. He wore a white suit and square shoes and carried a leather briefcase with brass accents. If Saffron had to guess, she'd say he was an accountant.

The door flapped gently and Saffron took hold of it and climbed the steps, calling, "Hello? Ms. Avery? Catering!"

"Come in, come in," Elyse called. Saffron climbed the steps into what felt like a whole different world.

It was as if someone had taken a suite from a luxury hotel —complete with hardwood floors, marble countertops, and leather sofas—and plunked it down on the beach. The windows had shades and curtains, there were regular dishes in a full-sized sink. A big-screen TV took up one corner of the living space, a dining-room table with carved chairs took up another.

Saffron was momentarily speechless. She held up the styrofoam container as Elyse descended a set of stairs from what seemed to be, from Saffron's glimpse, a bedroom. Elyse looked completely refreshed, radiant, and welcoming.

"Oh, Saffron," she said, as if they had known each other for years, "how kind of you to bring my dessert!"

"This trailer is amazing," Saffron said, unsure of whether saying so was within the bounds of etiquette.

Elyse waved a casual hand, "Eh. It's nice, but I much prefer your little cottage! It's so homey and cozy." Elise took a bite of her cheesecake, "Oh, man, I cannot get enough of this cheesecake! I sneaked some from the catering van this morning, and I've been craving it all day!" She popped the container open and snatched out the fork, diving into the cake with gusto.

"Sit, sit," Elyse said around her mouthful of cheesecake. She gestured toward the big leather couch, and Saffron sunk into it gratefully, enjoying the air conditioning and the sense of calm luxury in the trailer.

"You want something?" the star gestured toward the kitchen, but Saffron waved her off.

"No, no, thanks. I'm full of lobster."

Elyse wrinkled her nose, "Ew. Seafood sounds awful right now."

"It was actually delicious," Saffron began.

"Oh, I'm sure, I just don't like the sound of it. Anyway, this cheesecake is full of energy, and I'm going to need my strength for this next scene."

"Oh?" Saffron remembered glancing over the call sheet, but she couldn't remember what scene was filming this afternoon.

"Yeah. It's the meet-cute, and I have to carry that parrot around through a thousand takes."

"That's right," Saffron remembered, "Echo is making her debut on the big screen."

"If we can keep her from repeating everything she hears," Elyse rubbed her temples.

"Well, there's a reason her name is Echo."

"Rehearsals were rough," Elyse said, "First of all, she's a big bird, and by the time I've finished carrying her around for a couple hours, my back aches like crazy. Then, we had to keep going back because she'd say the same thing we'd just said over and over."

Saffron couldn't help but smile. Echo was a permanent fixture in the local pet shop: Barkadoodle. Saffron went in there a few times a month, and Echo always greeted her with enthusiasm.

There was a tap on the door, and Elyse said, "Oops, five minutes before I'm back on set. I guess I'd better get the rest of my costume."

Saffron stood to go, "Break a leg," she said. Elyse gifted her a smile as Saffron let herself back out onto the beach.

THE MEET-CUTE SCENE was all it was supposed to be: sweet, quirky, romantic, memorable. It began with Elyse and Adam sitting at what the set designers had transformed into a little beach cafe.

Saffron had lived in Maika'i long enough to know that

there was no cafe here on Shell Beach, but if she hadn't seen the uninterrupted stretch of golden sand so many times before, she would have been convinced by the building front, the servers, the umbrella-covered tables.

Saffron was surprised at how much difference there was between watching a movie being filmed and watching a movie in a theater. She couldn't hear most of the dialogue for this scene from where she stood, but she could see that the microphone technicians were close enough with their equipment to get the actors' voices loud and clear. She couldn't see every response or every expression, but the camera operators were set up just right to capture the trademark blink of Elyse Avery's lashes and the tense tapping of Adam Sullivan's heel.

What she did see clearly was Echo's big moment. The scarlet macaw made a rainbow streak through the air as she flew from Elyse's shoulder back to the arm of her owner and trainer, Bernie. The second film crew was all set up a little distance away, where Zayne stood waiting and started walking right on cue.

Echo, like a trained thief, swept down from the sky and grasped the fancy sunglasses he was wearing on his head. He exclaimed, then gave chase.

Saffron watched as he and Elyse wove through the extras and met, their ankles in the surf, as Echo landed back on the actress' shoulder and dropped the glasses into her hand. Saffron watched to see if she could see it from here—that spark, that giveaway that there was something special between the leading man and the leading lady.

And she saw it. Even from where she was standing, she saw the way he took her hand, the way his eyes searched her face, the way her body inclined toward his and the way she smiled at him like she had never smiled at anyone else before.

No question about it—the moment was magic.

Saffron had one more scene that afternoon. They shot it in the false cafe set. When Adam tried again to get Elyse to say "Yes," Saffron had to exclaim over the ring and offer to trade some shells for it.

Echo gave them fits throughout the scene. Regardless of her owner Bernie's instructions, she would not stay on the back of the chair near Elyse where she was supposed to be. Instead, she'd flap up onto an extra's head one minute, hop down to the table to sample the actors' food the next. She was especially excited about Elyse's salad. Once, she made three laps around the dining area, her enormous wings brushing cameras and bumping microphones, her tail smacking the actors.

It was too much for Adam. He leaped up, swearing, and stalked off the set. Echo landed on the back of his chair and helped herself to his club sandwich. It took the PA twenty minutes to calm him down and get him back to the set.

Even Saffron got to see Echo up close. Echo had always loved Saffron's red hair, and she landed on Saffron's shoulder twice during the whole fiasco.

Saffron liked Echo. She was kind of like an agile chicken. She could see that the big bird was anxious and that she was trying to do what people wanted her to do, but was unsure of what that was. Saffron stroked her and held up a strawberry, which Echo quickly dismantled with her powerful beak.

"Well, if you wanted her to be even more attracted to you," Bernie grumbled, coming over, "then mission accomplished. Now she's going to think that red hair really does mean sweet treats." Still he caught Saffron's eye and gave her a rare smile as he collected the parrot from her shoulder. She gave him back an understanding grin. Surprisingly, Elias Blum was incredibly patient with the bird. He simply called for another take, let them set up the shot again, and gave it another try—again and again.

"We can just do it without the bird," the Assistant Director suggested hopefully.

Blum was firm, "No, that will cause continuity issues. The audience will be asking themselves the whole scene, 'Where's the parrot?' instead of asking 'Is he the right guy for her?' which is what I want."

Saffron enjoyed seeing a little glimpse into Blum's process, and into his storytelling. He really did have a unique eye for it.

But Saffron could see that the cast and crew was getting frustrated.

"Um, Mr. Blum?" she said, raising her hand after one particularly disastrous take. Sitting at her cafe table, with her hand in the aire, she felt like she was in school again.

Jean the PA looked at her with murder in her eye. How dare she speak to the director? It was almost as bad as speaking to the principal actors.

Elias Blum, tangled around his chair, raised an eyebrow and gazed at her raised hand. She lowered it slowly.

"Yes, Gwen Thistledown?" he asked.

"Um. What if, I mean, would it work for the scene for Elyse to maybe give Echo a few treats while they're talking? Maybe some of those pumpkin seeds from her salad? She could just absentmindedly feed Echo the seeds, and I think that would keep Echo interested and still so you could get the shot."

There was a long silence, then Blum pointed at her, "See? This is why Gwen is an asset here," he said, looking around at his crew, "Gwen gets it. Gwen knows what we're here for. We're here to *get the shot*." He waved at Elyse, "Polly wants a cracker. Give it to her."

The next take went without a hitch on Echo's part. She kept focused on the treats, watching Elyse's hand as she picked a seed from the plate and held it up to the bird. Echo took them with great care, then watched for the next one. Though she swayed gently from side to side, bobbing her head with excitement, she stayed quiet and stayed on the chair.

When it came Saffron's turn to speak, she stepped back into Gwen's shoes and delivered her line as best she could. She hoped her performance was convincing enough for the audience.

It was certainly convincing enough for Slate and Mano. They cheered at the end, earning a scathing glance from the PA, but no commentary from the director. Finally being done after all those takes probably made him want to cheer, too.

When Saffron was released from the set, she walked over to them.

"You two!"

"Bravo!" Mano cried.

"Encore!" said her father, "You're a natural, Sunny!" he used her nickname from when she was a little girl.

"Oh, I don't know. It's not that hard. I just pretend to be someone else."

"That can be pretty challenging," Slate said with a twinkle in his eye. Saffron felt a pang. Slate had been in hiding with the witness protection program for three decades. He knew a thing or two about pretending to be someone else. Saffron smiled at him.

"You would know."

"I guess you get your acting chops from me," he didn't seem upset by the thought, or by the mention of his past. One thing she loved about hanging out with her father and Mano was their sense of perspective—they didn't get upset about too many things.

"And problem solving on the set, too!" Mano patted her shoulder, "I'm glad you were there for Echo."

Whether the bird heard her name or whether her arrival was simply coincidence, Saffron didn't get a chance to answer before a rainbow flash made her turn and brace. Echo sailed in for a smooth landing on her shoulder.

"Hi Echo," Saffron smiled, reaching up to stroke the big bird.

"Saffron! Saffron!" Echo knew her name and used it often.

Bernie came jogging up, his face a mask of fury, "Echo!" he scolded, "you can't go flying off like that!"

"Free bird!" Echo called. Saffron tried not to laugh.

"I've got to put you away and get back to the pet shop," Bernie said, "I've got a delivery of live fish coming any minute!" He rubbed his forehead, "I swear this movie, added to running the shop, is going to kill me off."

"I can take her back to her cage," Saffron said, "You go on back to the pet shop."

Bernie jumped at the offer, "Really? That would save me. Do you know where to put her?"

"Sure. I was in the makeup trailer this morning and I saw her cage."

Bernie thanked her profusely before scurrying off up the path toward the event center and the parking lot.

"That is really helpful of you, Sunny," Slate patted her arm, "you're always so good at supporting your friends."

"Uh-oh," Mano said.

Saffron turned to look at him quizzically. Echo's soft feathers brushed her cheek as she did so. "What?"

"I think me and your dad are going to have to buy some tuxedoes."

Saffron shook her head, confused, "why would you need tuxedoes?"

"To attend the award ceremony where you get 'best supporting actress."

Saffron rolled her eyes at the terrible joke.

"Awk!" Echo said, "Awful!"

Chapter Five

S late and Mano were going out to the egg farm to make some dinner. Saffron would follow after she deposited Echo in the trailer and returned her costume.

It was early evening, and the lights of Maika'i were strung like diamonds along the far end of the beach. The big movie lights had been shut off, the extras had gone home, even the stars' trailers were empty now. Saffron stood at the edge of the water, hearing the sounds of the set going to sleep—the clink of plates as the caterers packed up, the slam of van doors as the camera operators loaded their equipment for the night.

The evening was grapefruit pink and lilac, settling around Saffron. The heat had ebbed to a comforting warmth, chilled by a light breeze tickling its way up the sand from the sea.

Saffron felt it on her feet. It brushed her calves and made the hem of her borrowed sunwrap sway. Echo felt it too, and launched from Saffron's shoulder, winging her way out across the water in a big arc that brought her back to Saffron.

She did it again, and Saffron didn't scold her. It was beautiful watching her fly. She was grace and poetry in the air, beating her powerful wings and playing on the invisible currents. Saffron loved the bird for her wit and personality, but also for her brilliant colors. Echo's feathers lay in bright bands, and they were best seen when her wings were spread: crimson and cobalt, shamrock and butterscotch.

The sea, deepening to its night shades, matched the blue tips of Echo's wings, and when she dipped, trailing one wing in the surf, it looked as if she had emerged from the azure water, as if it had formed her and sent her skyward on the tip of a crashing wave, like sea spray.

The sun was a tangerine resting on the horizon, and it turned the sea orange around it. Echo sailed in front of it, making the kind of bird silhouette that Saffron used to draw in school—a little 'm' shape—before gliding back toward Saffron.

Saffron flipped her curls behind her shoulder, making a steady place for Echo to land. Echo had other plans, though. Excited by the taste of freedom, she sailed right past Saffron and flapped lazily off down the beach toward the sparkling lights of Maika'i.

Fear gripped Saffron's heart. What if Echo didn't come back? What if she got lost?

"Echo!" Saffron called, running after the parrot, "Echo, come back!"

The hala grove was a dark shape, reaching down nearly to the water. Saffron lost sight of Echo as the bird flew into the emerald shadows of the trees.

The sun was sinking fast now, and by the time Saffron reached the point of the grove, where the lapping waves brushed the pyramid roots of the hala trees, Echo was nowhere to be seen.

Saffron wished she had her cell phone, but it was back at the locker in the costume room.

"Echo!" she called, "Echo!"

The grove was dark and dense, and only occasionally could she see the stretch of apricot beach beyond. If Echo was in here, Saffron wouldn't be able to see her at all in a few more minutes.

She heard someone else calling, someone on the broad stretch of sand on the other side of the grove. Saffron struggled forward, the roots grabbing at her feet and costume, the light ebbing with every passing second. The leaves of the hala trees were drooping, pointed, and thick—a curtain of crocodile green that smelled bitter as Saffron pawed at it.

She fought through the last wall of leaves, enveloped in their shadow, and fell out onto the other side, directly into two strong arms.

"Whoa!" a deep, familiar voice rumbled next to her cheek. She looked up.

"Keahi!" involuntarily, reflexively, she hugged him. Keahi had been her first romance here, her best friend until he moved to Boston to resume his surgical practice. She'd seen him twice since then—once last month, when he'd returned at Saffron's request to perform a successful operation on a little girl in town, and once before that, on Christmas Day, when they'd shared a kiss on the beach.

Keahi hugged her back, his cheek against her hair. She heard him say her name with surprise.

Saffron found her footing, her heart making the same sound in her ears as the ipu heke, the double gourd drum used in hula dances. She straightened, pulling herself back, with great effort, from the comfort of Keahi's arms.

"What are you doing here?" she asked, "I thought you were in Boston."

Keahi didn't meet her gaze. He looked away, his eyes sliding to the sand. He was hiding something.

He fumbled to answer her question, "I'm—I'm just checking something out."

Saffron stepped back. There was something strange in his voice, "Checking what out?"

He sighed, heavily. "Look, Saffron, I didn't want to tell you this. I wanted you to hear it from the grapevine. Which, I guess, is totally unacceptable of me."

The drumming in her ears was growing louder, becoming a frantic rhythm over which she could barely hear.

"Evelyn wants to get married," he said the words, and then they couldn't be unsaid.

Images of his previous girlfriend, Evelyn, streaked through Saffron's mind. Evelyn was a nurse that worked with Keahi in Boston. They'd come, together, from the mainland to perform the operation on little Clara Tucker. In fact, Saffron had insisted he bring Evelyn, to ensure that Clara had the best chance at survival.

Now it was Saffron who couldn't meet *his* gaze. She looked past him, down the pristine beach, "You got back together? After you came here?"

Keahi's voice was tight, "you know what Hawaii does to people."

"So why are you here now?"

"She wants to get married here. Of course. And I said we could come down and check it out."

Saffron felt betrayed. Not only by Keahi. Mano was his grandfather, and he'd said nothing to her, though she'd seen him every day.

But the feeling didn't last long. Keahi was still talking, faster now, " . . . Can't say anything to Tutu, though, okay? I'm just here for a couple of days, and—what?" Their eyes finally met as he noticed she was staring at him.

"You haven't told Mano that you're here?" Saffron felt she was drowning in waves of various emotions. One minute she was excited, then hurt, the next, angry.

"Well . . . No. It's just a quick trip."

"You're not staying at home? What about your mom? Does she know you're here?"

"No, I told you, we just came down to scout some locations. No need to get everyone all involved," for the first time, Saffron really looked at him. Keahi, tall and handsome, with amber eyes and curly onyx hair, stood with his shoulders slumped, his usually smiling mouth pressed into a tight line.

"But, but," Saffron tried to find the words. Keahi was his mother's and grandfather's pride, the light in their lives. They planned every visit, looked forward to every moment they got to spend with him, "it would break their hearts to know you came home without seeing them."

Keahi, who was generally even and calm, was not now. "That's why you can't tell them," he snapped.

Saffron stepped back, making more space between them. "K?" she said, using the shortened version of his name that she'd adopted when they were dating.

Keahi softened, "Look, I don't like not telling them either, but Evelyn feels like we should keep it quiet a little while. She wants to decide where we're going to get married without any interference from my family. I get that. They are kind of pushy. You know how Tutu can be."

"I guess I wouldn't see it as pushy interference. It seems more like caring involvement."

"Depends on your perspective, I guess. She still hasn't really forgiven them for letting me stay the first time I came home."

"You mean after that first," Saffron stopped herself and tried to proceed delicately, "after the surgery went badly?" Keahi had lost a young patient in Boston and had come home to the island afterward. His family had supported him then, just as they'd supported him going back to Boston when he was ready.

"Yeah. That was the first time we broke up, and she never could understand why I walked away from being a surgeon for a while."

"Where is Evelyn?" Saffron asked, the name tasting bitter on her tongue.

"Back at her hotel," Keahi said, "resting from the flight."

"Her hotel?"

"Yeah. She's staying at the Little Hawaii resort."

"You're not?"

He shrugged, a guilty mask across his face, "No, I got too many friends working there. I'm staying up at the Silver Sands hotel up in Pali."

It was true. Several of the locals ran important parts of the Little Hawaii—the front desk, the pool, the breakfast buffet. They'd spot Keahi for sure, and word would get back around to his grandpa that he was here.

"It just doesn't seem like, you, is all," she said, searching his face, trying to get him to look at her.

He kept his eyes on the wall of greenery behind her, "Well, you know, maybe I've changed a little, being back in Boston."

"Maybe you've changed a lot."

Silence fell around them, like the darkness that was descending on the beach. Saffron felt wrapped in discomfort, in anguish, in anger.

When Keahi broke the silence, his voice seemed extra loud in the deepening evening, "What are you doing out here, anyway? In the hala grove?"

"I'm looking for Echo, you know, Bernie's parrot?"

"Yeah, I know Echo. I'm looking for her, too."

"What?"

"I was sitting on the beach with my keys beside me, and she swooped down, grabbed them, and flew off."

A bubble of laughter rose in Saffron's stomach, pushing aside her other churning feelings for a moment.

"It's not funny. That's a rental car. They'll charge me two hundred bucks if I don't get those back."

"It's a little funny," Saffron corrected him, giggling, "They probably have all kinds of people come in and say they left their keys in a restaurant or dropped them in the ocean, but can you imagine telling them that a parrot stole your keys?"

Keahi did not laugh. "What is Echo doing out of the pet shop anyway?"

"She's in the movie," Saffron said.

"Movie?'

"You haven't heard, then?"

Keahi shook his head. He really was out of touch. He must not have even been calling to visit with Mano lately if he didn't realize there was a movie filming in Maika'i. Mano surely would have told him all about it if they'd talked.

"There's a romantic comedy filming here in Maika'i. They started just over there on Shell Beach," she tipped her head toward the hala grove and the beach that lay beyond it, obscured by the dense trees. "Echo is the main character's pet. She's a pretty good actress." Saffron felt her stomach twist with worry. Where was Echo? How would she ever find the bird now that it was dark?

"Wow. I know a famous parrot," he peered at her through the dim light of the rising moon, "why are you the one chasing her through the dark?"

"Well, I was just finishing up on set and I said I'd put her away for Bernie, but she flew off."

"Finishing up on set? Are you in this movie?"

Saffron's face got warm, "Yes. I have a bit part."

"Wow!" Keahi sounded more like himself now, "I know a famous parrot and a famous girl."

"Famous may be a strong word for it," she shrugged, "and if I don't find that bird, I'm likely to be more infamous than famous. Not only is Bernie going to be upset, but if Echo's not back on set tomorrow, Elias Blum will completely freak out."

"Elias Blum?" Keahi's voice was high, "you're working with Elias Blum?"

"Working with him, avoiding him because he terrifies me, both are accurate."

"I'd love to see some shooting! Maybe I could drop by the set one day while I'm here?"

Saffron hesitated, battling an image of Evelyn hanging on Keahi's arm at the edge of the set, "Well, sure, you could. I mean, they haven't been too cranky about people watching from the sidelines," she took a deep breath, "but don't be surprised if you run into Tutu."

"Why? Is he in the film, too?"

"No, but he spent all day today watching the shooting."

Keahi breathed out, disappointment evident in his tone, "Well, it's my own fault I can't watch then, isn't it?"

Saffron didn't respond. The sound of the wind swishing the hala leaves behind them made up the space between their words.

"Well, I better go see if I can find that crazy Echo," Saffron said reluctantly.

"Echo! Echo!" the squawking refrain caused Saffron to look up. Above them, in a hala tree, was Echo. The bird glided down and landed on Saffron's shoulder. As she settled, she lifted a foot and dropped Keahi's keys into Saffron's hand.

"Where have you been?" Saffron scolded.

"Where have YOU been?" Echo echoed.

Saffron extended her hand, offering the keys to Keahi. When he took them, she tried not to feel the touch of his hand against hers, "I guess I'd better get her back into her cage," Saffron said. "It was good to see you." She wasn't sure that was true, but she wasn't sure it wasn't true, either.

"Yeah," Keahi shuffled his feet in the sand, "I'm, you know, I'm sorry about . . . everything."

"Take care, and good luck with . . . everything," Saffron turned and plunged back into the dark hala grove.

The set was dark except for a few safety lights, but the

events center where Saffron dropped off her costume and retrieved her things from the locker was still open and bright. The makeup trailer was unlocked, too.

Inside, Saffron flipped on the bright lights and noted that everything had been nicely tidied. She opened Echo's cage and held an arm inside so the big bird could step out onto the perch inside.

"Good night?" Echo asked.

"Yes, Echo. Good night. You go to sleep here."

"Bernie?" Echo asked. Saffron wondered for a moment if Echo had flown away earlier because she was looking for her master.

"Bernie will be back on set tomorrow," Saffron said. "Don't worry."

Echo hunched her shoulders in a pouty attitude. When she spoke, Saffron blinked. Her voice was almost a match to Bernie's. The tone was impatient, and the pitch was lower than Saffron had ever heard Echo speak before, "I'll be back, Echo. Good night, Echo."

Echo was obviously annoyed at Bernie for leaving her here overnight.

"It's okay," Saffron soothed, "you'll see him tomorrow." Saffron left a light on over Echo's cage. She moved toward the door, pausing as she opened it to glance back at Echo.

"Good night, Bernie," the parrot said to herself. Then, in Bernie's voice, she answered herself, "Good night, Echo."

"Good night, Echo," Saffron whispered as she stepped out and closed the door.

IT WASN'T until after Saffron put Echo away, after she drove out of the parking lot, after she saw Keahi driving away in his black rental car—a hilarious compact that would have seemed small on a toy-store shelf, much more so on the road—after she drove home, that she realized what awaited her there.

She was walking up to the back door when she heard voices and remembered that Mano and Slate were there, cooking dinner for her.

"There she is," Slate said as she came in. The two men were sitting at the kitchen table, a feast of huli huli chicken on a curly bed of rice noodles. Slate had been learning to cook lately, and he was getting very good.

Saffron looked past him, to Mano. His sweet, unassuming smile sent sea urchin spines through her chest. She had only been in the room with him for five seconds, and she already felt the guilt of lying to him. It only got worse as he spoke, "Get distracted on the way home?"

Saffron nodded, her mouth dry, "Echo flew off and I had to go find her."

Slate looked up in alarm, "Was she okay?"

"Yes," Saffron said, omitting the middle of the story, "she came back."

"Well, we've got your supper ready. You must be hungry after that long day on the set," Mano dished up a plate and pushed it toward her. As Saffron sunk into her chair, she suddenly realized how hungry and exhausted she was.

Sweet, smoky flavor filled Saffron's mouth as she took the first bite. The chicken was marinated in pineapple juice, ginger, soy sauce, and honey, then grilled between two racks. Huli meant 'turn' in Hawaiian, so the name reflected the style of cooking. Saffron had eaten lots of huli huli chicken since coming to Maika'i, but this one was different. There was a subtle flavor she didn't recognize.

"This is amazing," she praised them, relieved to have something truthful to say. "There's a new flavor. I can't identify it."

The two were smiling conspiratorially, "Guess," Slate said.

"Hmmm. Guava?"

They shook their heads.

"Cinnamon?"

Another shake.

"Wait. Is it . . . Cherry?"

"Bingo!" Slate was as proud of her guessing it as he was of the dish itself. "It's a little contribution from my years in Seattle —Rainier cherry juice added to the marinade."

"Wow, Dad, you're really getting good!" She took another bite, this time scooping some rice noodles. She noticed how Mano was watching her expectantly, which made it obvious he had been in charge of making the noodles. They were delicious —chewy and tender, drenched in a mild and creamy coconut basil sauce that was the perfect complement to the sweet and smoky chicken.

"These noodles are incredible!" she praised, "Tutu, you are a gourmet!"

He chuckled happily, and Saffron fixed her gaze on him for a moment. He was square, with sparkling eyes and a trim beard. His ever-present smile had created crescents of wrinkles that radiated out from the corners of his eyes. His face was open, honest, trusting.

Saffron felt the tears slipping down her cheeks and saw Mano's gaze follow them to where they dripped on the table cloth. His eyes registered concern.

"Mo'opuna?" he said gently, using the word for grand-daughter, "What is it?"

Saffron shook her head. She couldn't tell him. Not because Keahi had asked her not to, but because she couldn't bear to tell Mano that his grandson was in town and wasn't planning to see him. And because she couldn't bear to tell him why Keahi was in town, either.

Slate was watching her now, too, "Sunny, is something wrong?"

Something was wrong. Very wrong. But Saffron couldn't

say what. She couldn't say why she had to force herself to swallow her bite of chicken and why her appetite was gone. She couldn't say why the trickling tears turned to sobs.

Slate and Mano exchanged a look. It held concern and resolve.

"You need some rest," Mano said, "come on, now." He stood and took one of Saffron's hands. Her father took the other. Together, they walked her down the hall and sat her on the edge of her bed, "If you get some sleep, things will look better."

"We'll stay until you drift off," Slate said, "We'll be in the living room if you need us."

As they left the room Saffron tried her best to give them a smile.

Chapter Six

Curry woke Saffron with an tense bawking that she recognized as an alarm. She sat up. She was still in yesterday's clothes, and she padded down the hall in bare feet to peer out the front window for the source of Curry's consternation.

The sun had just broken over the wide stretch of water in front of the house, turning the row of palm trees into wallpaper silhouettes, crooked and comical. Another floral shape caught Saffron's eye, and she realized that out on her lanai, gracing the little patio table, was an enormous bouquet of flowers.

It was so big, in fact, that she didn't realize until she got outside that there was someone behind it.

Saffron's friend, the Empress, sat in her wheelchair on the other side of the table. She turned her kind eyes to Saffron.

"Empress!" Saffron went in for a kneeling hug. The empress, a large woman with ample arms, gave the best hugs. Saffron pulled back, careful of the little chirping chicken on the Empress' lap. Princess was a fluffy white silkie hen who lived a life of pampered luxury, riding around with the Empress wherever she went.

The Empress took Saffron's chin in her hand, "What is this I hear about you crying yourself to sleep?"

It all came flooding back—the movie set, the parrot, Keahi. Saffron slumped back on her heels, tears pricking her eyes again.

"Oh!" the Empress cried, as if stung, "This is serious!"

Saffron nodded miserably.

"First, I have brought you a gift." The Empress waved a hand at the table. Beside the enormous flower arrangement was a dress. Covered in a delicate blue and white floral pattern, the dress had a sweet a-line skirt, fluffy sleeves, and a sweetheart neckline. It was breezy and beautiful and made Saffron want to cry even more.

"Hang it in the bathroom to smooth the wrinkles out," the Empress said, "and then come right back here."

Saffron obeyed. She almost had her tears under control when she came back and knelt by the Empress again.

"Thank you," Saffron said.

"Now, my dear, you must tell me immediately what is wrong, and I will do everything I can to fix it," the Empress' warm brown eyes searched Saffron's face, and keeping the secret seemed completely impossible. Saffron was sure her friend could read the truth in her eyes.

"I can't," she choked out, "I can't tell you the truth."

"Of course you can!" the Empress dismissed the thought, "you can tell me anything, my dear."

"I can't."

"Of course you can."

Saffron looked around for the two strong, middle-aged men, Rex and Carlo, that the Empress employed as assistants.

"Where are Rex and Carlo?" Saffron asked softly. She couldn't let them hear what she was considering saying.

"Ah, they've gone for their morning run on the beach," the Empress waved her arm toward the water, "you don't need to worry about being overheard. Only Princess and I will hear your sorrow." She patted Saffron's shoulder, "And Princess is nothing if not discreet."

The woman's heavy hand stroked Saffron's cheek, and her gentle voice, with its beautiful Samoan accent, coaxed the secret from Saffron as naturally as a chick popped out from a hen's feathers.

"Keahi's back," Saffron said, her voice breaking on his name, "I met him on the beach last night."

The sound the Empress made was half sigh, half murmur, "I see, I see. And you are afraid that Nik will find out you've been seeing him?"

The words jolted Saffron. She hadn't even thought about Nik's reaction to all this.

"No, no, I haven't been seeing him."

"But you said you met him on the beach last night."

"Accidentally. I didn't even know he was back in town."

The Empress squinted at Saffron, then switched her gaze to the table behind them, "Those do not seem like the gift of someone who was met by accident."

Saffron looked at the flowers. They were exquisite—a

crescent of lilies, roses, plumeria and hibiscus. They sported a sticker on the side of the vase revealing that they were from The Sprout Shop, Holly's nursery and floral design business in Maika'i. Saffron was familiar with bouquets because of her event planning business—this one must have cost a fortune.

The thought gave her pause. Who *would* send her such a bouquet? It was definitely not Nik's style, and with Keahi's recent news, she was fairly certain it wasn't him, either.

"Nelson used to send me the most beautiful bouquets," the Empress sighed, "he had such exquisite taste." Saffron had never met the Empress' late husband, but if the tastefully-decorated mansion she lived in was any evidence, Nelson had indeed been discerning. "Let me tell you," the Empress went on, "a bouquet like that means something. It's meant for someone who is very, very special to the sender. I wouldn't be surprised if Keahi—"

"It's not from Keahi," Saffron said quickly.

"Well, how do you know?" the Empress chided.

Saffron blurted the words, let them spill out with abandon: "Keahi's getting married."

The Empress, never one of subtle reactions, gasped audibly. She said nothing, simply laid a hand to her heart and shook her head slowly, her eyes wide. Princess, always in tune with the Empress' moods, gave a disapproving growl.

Saffron nodded, "He told me on the beach last night. And I can't say anything to Mano, and neither can you, because Keahi hasn't even told *him* or his mom that he's in town."

"And because knowing that would break his heart," the Empress shook her head sadly.

It felt good to have spoken it out loud. Keahi was home. He was getting married. In the bright morning light both things still seemed horrible, and neither could be denied.

They might have sat pondering their misery all day, if a

small sound had not drawn Saffron's attention. It was a high, insistent chirp.

She knew it immediately—it was the sound of a chick, and not a very happy one.

"Just a minute," she said, standing. The Empress nodded gracefully.

Climbing down the steps of the lanai, Saffron saw her: a little smudge of wet black fluff. It was one of the new chicks she'd recently been given. They were a special breed: Kadaknath chickens. Their feathers, combs, legs, and even their bones, she'd heard, were a rich midnight black. The little chick was soaked with dew and chirping its displeasure with gusto.

"How did you get out here?" Saffron asked. The little chick was supposed to be in the henhouse with its adoptive mother, Cupcake. "Don't you know anything could happen to you out here?" Saffron pushed away images of mongooses and scorpions and other predators.

"What is it?" the Empress called, a hint of worry in her voice.

Saffron leaned down and scooped up the little chick, holding it aloft in two protective hands. It was so light that she barely felt it. The only indications she had that it was there was the dampness in her palms and its fluttery breathing.

"Oh, my!" the Empress' delight was immediate and obvious, "bring the little darling here! Oh, immediately!" In her excitement, she wheeled her chair a few inches closer to Saffron, something the Empress nearly never did.

Saffron knelt down and held the little creature close so the Empress could see it.

But it was not the Empress who was most interested. Princess raised her head and leaped to her feet. At first, Saffron was afraid—some hens would attack chicks that were not their own—but it quickly became obvious that Princess was feeling affectionate, not aggressive. She purred and clucked and the little chick perked up, crying even more loudly. Princess reached for it, and before Saffron could stop it, the little chick had leaped from her palm and run to the silkie, nestling under Princess' downy white feathers.

The Empress could not have been more overjoyed, "Oh, look at how she attends to the little thing!" Princess was carefully stroking the chick's feathers, craning her neck and lifting her wing as the chick reached a beak up toward her with sad little squeaks.

Princess crooned and preened, dried and fluffed the chick. Silkie chickens had a reputation for being exceptionally maternal, and Saffron saw that now in Princess.

When Saffron glanced up at the Empress, she saw tears in the woman's eyes.

"This is the most perfect little creature," the Empress said, "what an incredibly sweet angel!"

It was true. The little chick could not have looked more innocent and adorable. Snuggled up against Princess' fluffy white feathers, she looked like a little smudge of soot.

"I've been calling her Duchess," Saffron replied.

The Empress' eyes widened, "It's meant to be," she said solemnly.

"Hmmm?" Saffron mused, still trying to push the thought of Keahi away.

"Saffron," the Empress announced. The solemnity and gravity of her tone made Saffron pay attention, "I would like to buy this chicken."

Saffron blinked, "I'm sorry, what?"

"How much? Thousands? Anything you ask."

Saffron looked at the chick and Princess, perfectly content together. She looked at the Empress, gazing down at the duo with affection. She thought about her new friend, Mr. Phule, who had given her the little chick. She felt sure that he, of all people, would understand.

"Don't be ridiculous," she finally said, "of course. That little one belongs with you two."

"I will pay any amount," the Empress was rarely this passionate, never this desperate.

Saffron took the woman's hand, "I wouldn't take a penny. She's yours."

The Empress made a little squeal and gathered the chick into her hands, "Do you hear that? You will be a part of our family now!"

* * *

THERE WAS no card on the flowers. Saffron's best guess was that they were from her father and Mano. When she stopped in at the Sprout Shop on her way to the set that morning, though, Holly gave her a surprise: the flowers were from Zayne Grayson.

"Zayne Zayne? The actor?" Saffron felt a cool breeze from the refrigerated room where Holly was extracting freshly-delivered flowers from long boxes and placing them in big tubs of water. The breeze was a grandma's perfume: carnations and roses and something else Saffron couldn't identify. The room was a dance of pink and green, delicate lilac and bold fuchsia. Saffron soaked in the colors, picking out the ones that had been in her bouquet: hydrangea, lisianthus, some kind of peach and cream rose. There were hundreds of flowers in here, and Holly needed to get them all into their tubs before she opened the shop for the day. Saffron started pulling bunches of flowers out of the boxes, snipping their stems, and placing them in tubs marked with their names: sunflowers, lilies, daisies.

"Not a lot of other Zaynes in town, are there?" Holly said, shrugging. She had dyed her very short hair into a series of black and orange tiger stripes, and they shifted and bounced as she spoke.

Saffron blinked, "But why . . . Why would he send me flowers?" she contemplated a handful of orchids, trying to figure out if they were dendrobium or phalaenopsis.

Holly gestured to the tub on her right, the dendrobium, then looked at Saffron pointedly, "Tell me you aren't that naive?"

"What do you mean?" Saffron slid the orchids into their tub.

Shifting, Holly rolled her eyes toward the ceiling, "Well, you know the old saying about sailors having a girl in every port?"

"Wait a minute," Saffron held up her hands.

"Well, Zayne Grayson is rumored to have a girl on every set," Holly lifted an enormous bunch of long-stemmed roses from a box and peered through it at Saffron, "the tabloids say that's why he's never seen with anybody in particular on the red carpet—he's not interested in a long-term relationship."

"Even if that's true," Saffron said defensively, "I'm not the girl. I've barely said two words to him."

"Maybe he's trying to change that," Holly said, her eyebrows bouncing up and down behind the red bells of the roses, "and woo you."

"I doubt it," Saffron said, "he's probably just sending them as a thank-you for my hospitality letting them stay in the cottages."

Holly's brown eyes snapped, "No way. I've seen 'thank you' bouquets. They're 40, 50 dollars, maybe a hundred. That work of art on your lanai was over four hundred."

"Four hundred dollars?"

Holly nodded, "Yep. Pushing five."

"Wow," Saffron opened another box, extracting bunches of lemon-yellow and berry-purple flowers with multiple layers of delicate petals.

"I know."

"But I have a boyfriend," Saffron pictured Nik's tousled hair, his green eyes.

Holly scoffed, "Oh, please. Nik's great and all, but if you have to choose between him and Zayne Grayson?" she bunched up her face, "No question."

"I'm not sure about that. I don't even know Zayne. And if he's got a girl on every set? Pass." Saffron dropped the flowers into a tub marked *peonies*.

"That's ranunculus!" Holly said.

"No it's not. I'm not about to break up with Nik just because—"

Holly shook her tiger-striped head and pointed at the tub in front of Saffron. "Not ridiculous. Ranunculous. Those flowers aren't peonies. They're ranunculous."

Saffron snatched the bunches back out and dropped them in the right bucket, "*You're* ranunculous if you think I'm going to let Zayne Grayson breeze in here and sweep me off my feet like a girl in one of his movies."

Holly narrowed her eyes at Saffron, "*You're* ranunculous if you don't at least give him a shot. What could it hurt to talk to him? Get to know him?"

Saffron didn't have a reply.

"Don't mess it up," Holly pointed a finger at Saffron, "I could use more of his business."

"I always make my important life decisions based on your financial situation," Saffron said, "regardless of the emotional investment of the man in question."

"Hey, he seemed pretty invested—he selected every flower by hand."

That gave Saffron pause. She'd assumed he called in the order, "If he's so interested, why didn't he write a card?"

"Maybe that's part of his game. Just get you interested, then a big reveal?"

Saffron sighed, "This whole thing is ranunculous."

THE CONVERSATION WAS on her mind later, when she was making her way down Shell Beach toward the set. The rising sun was molten gold and where it touched the water, it had turned gold, too. The waves lapped her feet. The popping bubbles left behind every time the water receded made a gentle music.

She was watching the bubbles when she glanced up and saw a figure walking down the beach toward her. His square shoulders, the swagger, and the clean line of his jaw all told her that it was Zayne.

She thought about ducking into the underbrush beside the beach, but he'd already seen her. He raised a hand and waved, and Saffron had no choice but to wave back.

"Beautiful morning," he called out as he drew closer.

"It is," she agreed. She found her cheeks burning, found it hard to look him in the eye.

"Your cottages are beautiful, too," he said, stopping. Saffron lost any hope she had that he would just walk on down the beach. She was going to have to have a conversation with him.

"I'm glad you're finding them comfortable," she said.

Zayne was a man used to the effect he had on women. Saffron could tell by the way he stepped close and made direct eye contact when he spoke. She could tell by the way he angled his shoulders toward her.

"Very. Listen, though, Miss Skye," he leaned in, close enough that Saffron could smell the sharp scent of the cologne he was wearing. She wondered briefly if it was the one named after him, "I wonder if I could, maybe, come visit you in your bungalow later today?"

Here it was. The big reveal Holly had mentioned. Zayne was going to tell her he was interested, maybe make a move.

"Well, I don't know," Saffron blinked to clear his blue eyes from her mind for a moment, "I'm pretty busy all day, I mean, I don't know how long I'll be on set, and my *boyfriend*," she emphasized the word, "may be coming by later."

"Of course," he said, but didn't back away as she thought he might, "it would only take a moment. I, well, I need to pick something up."

"Pick something up?" she asked, "From my bungalow?"

Zayne ducked his head, shrugging mischievously, "I bought some flowers that I want to give to someone. They should be delivered to your house sometime today."

"Flowers?" Saffron was beginning to see her error.

"Yes, a huge bouquet. The paparazzi has been all over me this entire trip, and when I went to buy them at the local flower shop, there were paparazzi everywhere. I couldn't walk out with them and expect to go unnoticed, so I just had them delivered to your house so I could pick them up when nobody was watching."

"Of course," Saffron was relieved, but, to her surprise, she found she was also a little disappointed. Some part of her had been flattered by the thought that Zayne Grayson might be trying to woo her, "They were actually delivered this morning, and I put them inside on the table. The house is unlocked. You can feel free to just go in and get them whenever it's convenient for you."

"Thank you," his appreciation was genuine. For the first time, Saffron noticed a weary tightness in the movie-star smile he wore. "It's hard being watched all the time."

Sympathy tugged at Saffron's heart, "I can imagine," she said, "it must get very old."

Zayne's gaze was more sincere, more genuine, than Saffron had expected from a superstar. He looked, suddenly, like a regular person. An incredibly handsome and poised and charming regular person, but a regular person with feelings and reactions like everyone else's. "You can't do anything, not really, without your motives and the implications being scrutinized. I eat chocolate cake in a restaurant, people think I'm bulking up for a role. I drink a smoothie, people claim I've gone vegan. I take a drive in my car, people say I've snapped and am running away to the country."

Saffron made a sympathetic noise, but didn't try to say more. She let Zayne keep speaking, and as he began to walk along the beach again, she walked beside him, listening. He seemed to need a friend, a listening ear, a human connection. If Hawaii had given her anything, it had given her the ability to appreciate people and treat them with aloha.

"I started acting when I was eight. A commercial here, a bit part there. By the time I was fifteen, I was starring in a sitcom, then moved to the big screen in my early twenties. For over two decades I've been in movies, and for my whole life I've been dodging paparazzi, hiding from cameras, trying to slip past reporters. I've lived like a criminal, afraid to go out because someone might recognize me."

Saffron murmured to show him she could imagine that strain. It made her think of her father, who had been in the witness protection program for three decades, living someone else's life, afraid to be recognized. When, a few months ago, he had helped nab the criminals who were threatening his life, he'd finally been able to live again.

"Couldn't you tell them you didn't want to be in the spotlight?" she asked, "I mean, couldn't you legally get them to leave you alone?"

"Impossible. They don't quit. They're like tigers, just skulking in the shadows, waiting to jump out and snap your most embarrassing mistakes, your most private moments," he was more agitated now, kicking up little puffs of sand as he walked, "I can't have a normal relationship, can't even go visit my mother without wearing a disguise, can't eat out." He turned toward her abruptly, snatching her hands in his.

Saffron tried not to let her heart flutter at the touch of his strong fingers, at the intensity in his eyes, at the way he stepped close to her.

"You're lucky, you know?" he said, his ice-blue eyes boring into hers, "so lucky, to have a regular life and regular friends, regular days."

Saffron was about to agree with him when, along the stretch of sun-warmed sand, the clicking sound of a shutter resonated.

Zayne spun around, one hand still clutching Saffron's. More shutter clicks. Saffron saw the flash of a lens in the foliage behind them.

"Rossi!" Zayne shouted. There was fury in his voice. Every muscle in the star's shoulders and neck were tensed. He took a step toward the bushes where the photographer must have been hiding.

Saffron imagined the headlines: STAR GOES NUTS ON HAWAIIAN BEACH or ZAYNE GRAYSON THROWS PHOTOGRAPHER INTO THE OCEAN.

Zayne seemed like such a nice guy. She didn't want him splashed all over the news because of some jerk photographer. She reached up and put her free hand on his shoulder, pulling him back, cooling his anger.

It seemed to work. He relaxed, turning back toward her with a pleading expression, "See what I mean?"

She nodded, "It must be awful."

When she looked again, the glint of the lens was gone.

"That guy is the worst," Zayne fumed, walking a few steps away from her, back toward the set.

"You know who it is?"

"Sure. Rossi. A photographer who's been chasing me for years. He used to shoot other people, too, but he's become obsessed with me. I swear he has nothing else in his life besides photographing me."

Saffron followed Zayne back up the beach.

"I needed a little break from the set. That's what I get for trying to feel like a human for a minute."

As Saffron watched him walk toward his trailer, she was glad she'd gotten to see him as more than an actor, as a human, for a minute.

Chapter Seven

The set was sleepy this morning. The only activity seemed to be around the catering tables, where an appealing breakfast sent the aroma of ham and pancakes drifting across the beach.

Saffron knew her call time was early. She didn't have time for breakfast. She needed to get to the makeup trailer and be sure that Gwen Thistledown would appear right on cue. So she set off across the beach, up through the hala grove, and into the parking lot.

The door to the makeup trailer was closed, but Saffron pushed her way in without really thinking about it. Her mind was still on Zayne and the paparazzi. It was the last moment of distraction she would have.

The trailer was still. Too still. A figure lay on the floor. Saffron rushed over and dropped beside Shar, who lay on the floor between the makeup chairs, the bright lights over the mirrors illuminating her hair like a hedgehog-spiked halo.

Saffron didn't say her name. There was no need. Shar lay on her stomach, one arm out behind her, another tucked underneath her. One of the woman's false eyelashes had come loose and was stuck to her red-tinted cheek. Shar was dead.

Saffron pulled out her phone. She spoke more softly than she otherwise might have.

"Call Officer Bradley," she said.

When the familiar voice spoke at the other end of the line, Saffron explained where she was and what she was looking at.

"Don't touch anything," Bradley said, "I'll be there just as soon as I can." As the only officer in the little town of Maika'i, he was often needed in two places at once.

Saffron hung up and stayed sitting on the floor. A sudden, loud voice made her jump.

"What are you doing?" Echo accused from her cage. Her tone was angry.

"It's alright, Echo," Saffron said, "It's alright."

"Get out of here!" Echo screamed. "Get out of here!"

Saffron glanced up. The parrot wasn't sitting on her perch serenely as she often did this early in the morning. She was hanging upside down, climbing across the bars at the top of her cage. Echo used her powerful beak to swing down, then back up again, bobbing her head in agitation.

"What are you doing? Get out of here!"

A sudden chill, like a cold breeze, gripped Saffron. Echo's voice was different than usual. It was terrified, angry. Was the bird giving her a warning?

Saffron rose to her feet and looked around.

There were no signs of a struggle. Though one chair was turned all the way around to face the door, and there were two palettes of makeup spread on the counter, their accompanying little bottles of spirit gum and setting spray strewn about them on the floor and on the counter, it was not a scene of chaos or horror. Other than the body on the floor, the trailer looked about how it had looked every other time Saffron had been inside.

"Get out of here!" Echo screamed.

Saffron made a soft shushing sound, trying to calm the bird, "It's okay, Echo. I'm just going to look around a little."

What had happened?

Was Shar's death a random occurence? Or had something more sinister happened to the woman? Now that Shar's face was relaxed, Saffron could see wrinkles and lines that indicated maybe the woman was older than she'd first seemed. Her death could have been a totally natural event.

Saffron gazed around the trailer. She inspected the two makeup kits: Shar's and Roman's. She peered at the call sheets that lay on the counter between the open kits. They would tell her who else might have come by for makeup early this morning.

The first name gave her chills—Zayne Grayson. She had just spoken to him, and she had seen the flare of his temper.

Another name: Ace Carnation.

Ace? Though Saffron hadn't seen him yet today, she wasn't about to rule him out.

Two more names: Adam Sullivan—the other man—and Elyse Avery. All the principals had appointments. Any one of them might be a suspect.

But why? What possible motivation could any of them have for killing the head makeup artist in the middle of the shoot? That would only delay the film and surround it with controversy.

Controversy. She remembered what Ace had said: Any press is good press. Ace didn't mind being thought badly of, as long as he was thought of. Perhaps he felt the same way about the movie. If something horrible happened on the set, it was likely to drive an increase in box-office sales.

Saffron shook the thought from her head. Was she becoming too jaded?

She opened a cupboard. All seemed in place there, though

truthfully she wouldn't necessarily know if something was missing.

She needed to talk to Roman. He would know if anything had been moved. She ran her eyes over the shelves, trying to memorize their contents. Hairspray, inserts for the makeup kits, wipes, cotton balls and cotton swabs, sponges, bottles of unidentified liquids, everything one would need to make up the stars.

"Saffron," the word was drawn out with disapproval, a warning.

Saffron turned around to see the heavy gaze of Officer Bradley. He was shaking his head.

"I didn't touch anything," Saffron said defensively, closing the cupboard.

"I'll bet you didn't," Bradley shot her a doubtful look as he crouched beside Shar. Saffron had been known to tamper with evidence if the need arose. "Who's this?"

"She's the makeup artist. Her name is Shar. I don't know much about her."

"Hmm," he looked up, "that's unusual."

"I do have a life of my own, you know," Saffron said, "I don't spend every waking moment sleuthing."

"I know that," he said, "some of them you spend starring in major motion pictures." He was teasing her. She'd come to like and respect Bradley. She even appreciated his gruff exterior.

"I wouldn't say *starring*," she said.

"So, what's the scoop? Angry ex? Jealous assistant? Bitter starlet whose makeup failed to cover her blemishes?"

Saffron shrugged, "I have some ideas, but we should consider the possibility that maybe she just died."

Bradley laughed, "What is this, backwards day? I'm usually the one who says stuff like that."

"Maybe I'm just trying to think the best."

He grunted, "Well, I guess we'll let Arlene—the medical examiner—give us those answers." He spoke into the radio on his shoulder for a moment while Saffron ran her eyes over the scene once again.

Before Saffron could answer him, a gasp from the doorway drew her attention. Jean Beal, the production assistant, was standing on the steps, her eyes wide, "What in the world?"

Bradley rose, putting himself in Jean's line of sight, "I'm sorry, ma'am, but you'll need to back off a few paces. This is an active crime scene."

"No," Jean said, struggling with her words, "No it's not. It's the makeup trailer. I'm supposed to get the bird and Gwen Thistledown out of here and down on the set," she glared at Saffron.

Bradley looked from her to Saffron.

"That's me," Saffron explained, "I mean, that's my character."

He gestured toward the door, "Well, you'd better go. Your audience awaits."

"But don't you need—"

"You know, twenty years as a police officer has given me some experience. I think I can handle an investigation without the local egg farmer."

Saffron felt torn. He was right. The only reason she wanted to stay was because of her sharp curiosity. He didn't need her. She took a step toward the door, but was stopped by Jean Beal's sharp voice, "Bring the bird, too!"

Saffron stepped gingerly past Shar's still form and opened Echo's cage. The macaw cowered in the back corner.

"Hey, hey," Saffron crooned, "It's okay." She reached into the cage toward the trembling bird.

"Get out of here!" Echo screamed again. Saffron was about to withdraw her arm when, without warning, Echo leaped for it, grasping her forearm and clambering up to her shoulder with an almost maniacal intensity.

Echo ducked under Saffron's long red hair, tucking her beak into Saffron's neck, just below her earlobe.

After last night, Saffron was slightly nervous to step out of the trailer with Echo. She was afraid the big bird might get distracted and wing her way off into the blue again, but Echo's response was quite the opposite. The parrot clung to Saffron, her soft head brushing Saffron's cheek as they walked. Occasionally, she would squawk, "Get out of here!"

The principals were on set when they arrived. Elyse stood laughing with Adam under an enormous umbrella while Ace leaned far too close to one of the assistant directors.

Saffron looked around for Zayne and spotted him beside Elias Blum's chair. She couldn't help but notice that he looked grim. Was that because of Rossi the photographer or was something else bothering him? Saffron tried not to speculate.

Mano and Slate were in their usual place off on the edge of the beach, and Saffron drew comfort from seeing them there. She also smiled because next to them was another familiar face: the Empress, complete with Princess and Duchess.

Elias Blum was so focused on the scene he was shooting that he didn't pay any attention to the onlookers.

"There's the bird!" he cried as Saffron approached with Echo, "Now we can get going!"

Saffron spent the next few hours walking on and off the set, saying her few lines over and over, and eyeing every person in the vicinity.

I'm sure she died of natural causes, Saffron thought after the fifth take, when Adam went to get Elyse a folding chair and got reprimanded by Zayne for leaving the set, *there's no need to suspect anyone here.*

She wanted to call Bradley, wanted to ask if the medical

examiner had said anything yet, but she was stuck in an endless loop of retakes.

A ruckus near the director's chair caught her attention. She watched as Roman rushed up and explained to Blum that Shar was dead.

"Are you kidding me?" Blum wrapped an arm even tighter around his chair. Saffron thought the chair might snap like kindling from the pressure.

"And the hillbilly policeman won't allow me into the trailer at all—I can't get to any of my supplies!" Roman fumed.

"No makeup?" Blum demanded, "Is that what you're telling me? This could set us back days!"

Saffron felt they may be focusing on the wrong points here.

"I know, sir," Roman sounded like a wheedling weasel, "but there's nothing I can do. The closest supplier is back in LA."

"You're telling me there's no makeup on this whole island?"

"Well, no, sir, but I have no idea where—"

"Gwen Thistledown!" Blum shouted her name so abruptly that Saffron flinched.

Blum was waving her over. Saffron hustled across the sand as quickly as she could.

"Gwen," Blum's voice was commanding, "you're a woman. You wear makeup. You live here. Take my car," Blum flipped her his keys, "and my makeup man here, and show him where to buy some makeup in this town."

Roman looked at Saffron in horror, "It won't be the right kind," he said, "we use only the best—"

"Do you have any idea how much every minute of production is costing?" Blum asked, acid in his voice. He didn't wait for an answer, "Of course you don't. That's my job. But let me tell you, you'll find some makeup and you'll make do, or I'll make sure you never work in film again."

BLUM'S CAR WAS A RENTAL, but it was unlike any rental Saffron had ever seen. It was a cherry-red sports car, gleaming with chrome and leather, a convertible. The wind blew her long red hair as they drove to the Paradise Market. Roman was mumbling as they pulled into the parking lot.

They left half an hour later with two reusable cloth grocery bags. Saffron had, on a whim, bought copies of all the celebrity gossip magazines. Roman held a bag full of foundation, eyeliner, shadows, blushes, highlighters, and lipsticks. Roman had uttered disparing phrases so often during their shopping trip that Saffron had been afraid he would have some sort of melt-down. "I think you'll be pleased with the durability, at least," Saffron tried to reassure him.

"If I was after durability, I'd just use permanent markers," he countered, "Asking me to subtly contour a cheek with this," he lifted the bag and held it toward her, wearing an expression like it was full of dead fish, "is like asking Da Vinci to paint the Mona Lisa using pudding."

Roman didn't seem to recognize that he was gifted at exaggeration, so Saffron stifled her giggle. She, for one, would pay good money to see the Mona Lisa recreated in pudding. Roman lowered the bag, holding it away from himself. Saffron allowed him to ride in sullen silence for a moment before asking, "It's terrible about Shar, though."

Roman's eyelids fluttered briefly, "Terrible," he repeated.

"When did you last see her?" Saffron asked.

He glanced over at her, a guarded look crossing his features, "last night, of course, when we put everything away."

This surprised Saffron.

"You weren't there this morning?"

"No, Shar insisted on doing the big stars before I got there, and before the bit parts showed up. She was mortified that you and Adam Sullivan were in the chairs at the same time before."

"Mortified?" Saffron felt a little offended.

"Surely you realize that a star like him shouldn't be attended to in the same vicinity as amateurs like yourself."

"I'm going to pretend I do realize that so that you'll stop looking so disgusted," Saffron said.

"It's no offense, girl," Roman held up his hands, "it's just how it is. Hollywood has a hierarchy. The stars are the royalty. The rest of us are the peasants. The faster you realize that, the happier you are in this business. Shar knew that." Saffron listened for a tremble in his voice, for a moment of emotion as he contemplated his boss's passing, but she heard none. "Take me, for example. I've been the underling for my entire career, cowering in Shar's shadow. Now, I can move into the spotlight. It wasn't my turn to rule the trailer before, but now it is. I've ascended to the makeup throne, and from now on I won't be unseated. Even after this movie, I'll be able to rule the trailer, make up the stars, and get an assistant of my own."

A little alarm bell went off in Saffron's head: *Motive!*

"So, would you say you and Shar, you know, didn't get along?" Saffron asked delicately.

"Nobody got along with Shar," he said, then leaning over conspiratorially, "except for Blum, if you know what I mean."

"I do not," Saffron clarified.

Roman huffed out a big sigh, "oh, ask anyone. They were an item. Dating, courting, wooing. Blum had finally leaked a bit of their relationship to the magazines, and Shar was hearing wedding bells."

"But," Saffron's forehead hurt, and she realized she was scrunching her eyebrows together hard, "When you told him, he was only worried about the makeup. I didn't see him weep or wail or take a deep breath, or anything."

"Blum? Of course not. He's on set. Everything's about the movie. He has no personal life when he's working. Maybe he'll react tonight, or maybe not until he's done shooting this and back on the mainland. He has incredible emotional control."

"I'm not sure if that's control of emotion or lack of it," Saffron said.

"Oh, honey, don't fool yourself into thinking Blum and Shar had any great romance. They weren't meant for each other or anything. He admired her work, she admired his. They were spending time together, they weren't history's greatest love story."

Saffron felt sad about that. She felt sad that Shar had died, and sad that nobody seemed all that upset about it, and sad that she and Blum didn't have history's greatest love story. Saffron was beginning to wonder if there were any happy endings besides the ones Blum manufactured on the big screen.

Chapter Eight

The next morning Saffron's cell phone buzzed its way off the nightstand, waking her as it crashed to the hardwood floor.

She rolled over, fishing for it with one arm over the edge of the bed, and finally caught it. She had six texts and three voicemails.

With a growing sense of dread, she opened the first and second texts, both from Holly:

I told you so!!!
Call me and dish!!!

Saffron had no idea what that was all about. Her next text, from Nik, was equally cryptic.

I guess we need to talk, huh?

"Talk?" Saffron said aloud, "About what?"

The fourth text was a single period from the Empress. The fifth and sixth, each half of the word, "Moving," though it took a moment for Saffron to decipher that from:

Mo
and
ving

Knowing that the small keypad of the Empress' cell phone often caused the lady much frustration, Saffron went to her voicemail, expecting the Empress to have given up on the texts and opted for a phone call.

She was not disappointed. The Empress' warm voice and round accent made up the first message.

"Moving on is good for the soul. I know this is a hard time for you, but you are handling it beautifully!"

The other two voice messages were even more strange. One was from someone with the Associated Press, and the other from the Honolulu news outlet. Both were interested in speaking with her. Both would appreciate a call back at her earliest convenience.

It wasn't until Saffron walked into her front room in her

pajamas and saw the round lenses of five or more cameras pressed to the glass of her windows that she knew something very strange was going on.

Scrambling back down the hall, she heard Curry bawking a panicked warning call from outside. Feet thumped on her lanai, scuffing along the wrap-around boards. People were peering in her kitchen window. Saffron ducked into the bathroom and closed the blinds. Heart pounding, she climbed into the bathtub fully clothed and drew the shower curtain, too, just to be sure they couldn't see her.

She texted Mano and her father: *Photographers everywhere! Stay away from the egg farm!* Though her dad's days of hiding with the witness protection program were behind him, a media frenzy might still make him very uncomfortable.

It made *her* uncomfortable. What in the world did the paparazzi want with her? They couldn't be so hard up for news that they were chasing the landlords of celebrities now, could they?

She opened her phone and navigated to her email. Maybe she had missed an announcement that today was a publicity day for the movie and everyone in it would be bombarded?

But that wasn't it. They weren't interested in her rental prowess or her bit part.

Splashed across the internet, where Saffron ran into it as a "This might interest you" suggestion, was her own face peering out from behind Zayne Grayson on the beach yesterday.

The cropping suggested she was peeking out from behind him. Her hand was on his shoulder, and the headlines read, "Zayne's Secret Love!"

Saffron couldn't breathe. She clicked on one link and scrolled down, speed-reading the article, which claimed that Zayne had a secret relationship he'd been hiding, and that he'd gotten his girlfriend a part in the new film.

There were other photos: her on set, her driving in Blum's

car with her hair flying in such a way that you could see the back of Roman's head, but nothing else. In the context of the article, it could be assumed that she and Zayne were taking a drive down the shoreline.

But one photo completely shocked even Saffron herself. Though she remembered the moment, she certainly didn't remember it like this: she and Zayne, holding hands on the beach, leaning close, the sun rising behind them. From the angle, it looked as if they were kissing.

Nik.

The thought streaked across her mind. No wonder he felt they needed to talk. She dialed his number with shaking hands.

No answer.

She dialed Holly.

"Saffron! You vixen!" Holly was, obviously, delighted by the whole situation.

"No!" Saffron cried, her voice muffled by her pajama sleeve, "You don't understand."

"I understand that you took my advice!" Holly crowed, "And made the smart call."

"No! No calls. I didn't make a call. This is all fake—manu-factured—lies."

"Lies?" Holly's voice was subdued now, and Saffron could tell that her friend was disappointed.

"That's right. I ran into Zayne on the way to the set yester-day. We talked for just a few minutes. This photographer was hiding in the bushes, I didn't think anything of it. There are paparazzi everywhere! They are looking in my windows!"

Holly perked up, "Really? Well that's something, anyway. To the world, you're Zayne's mysterious lover, even if you aren't really."

"You have to send someone! I'm telling you, I'm hiding in my bathtub right now."

"You're in the bathroom? Great! At least you can get your

makeup on and scrunch that curly red hair before they get a shot of you ducking out to your car and zooming to the set to meet Zayne."

Half of that advice seemed sound. Saffron reached a hand out and snagged her makeup bag off the counter, then balanced it on her lap while she got ready. Maybe they'd be gone when she got out.

"Someone was killed on set yesterday, Hol," she said, holding her mouth open while she dabbed on some lip gloss, "Or died, anyway."

Holly's usual bubbly timbre was replaced with a somber tone, "Oh, no. That's terrible. Who was it?"

"The makeup artist," Saffron told her a bit about the woman, all that she knew, really, except for the part about her involvement with Blum. It seemed too intimate a detail to just go repeating, too much like gossip.

"Wow," Holly's voice was awed, "busy day for you yesterday."

"I'll say," Saffron picked up her brush and looked over her palette. Her makeup paled in comparison with that in the kits back on set. She had only a few colors of shadow, really only one foundation. It was in the bottom of her makeup bag that she discovered it, an old container of blush, dried and cracked from neglect. She found her complexion was generally ruddy enough to avoid using the stuff.

It was a warm peachy color, and she'd never liked the artifice it lent to her features, which were quiet theatrical enough, she thought. But its glare from the bottom of the bag caught her attention.

Blush. Red. Minium.

"Holly, I'm sorry. I gotta go. I gotta call Bradley."

She hung up before Holly could say goodbye.

Before she called Bradley, she looked up the mineral she'd seen in Colorado: minium. Yes, it was highly toxic.

Notwithstanding its use as a pigment, the mineral was a type of lead.

"Poison?" Bradley sounded doubtful.

"Yes. Lead poisoning. Have them check for it. I think that Shar's makeup had a mineral called minium in it. It's a . . . " Saffron read the screen of her phone for a moment, "a lead tetraoxide. Very toxic."

"Listen, Saffron, my wife wears blush that's almost as garish, and I'm sure she's not getting poisoned."

"This is different," Saffron said, "I've seen blush on thousands of people over my lifetime, and I've never seen *that* color in makeup before. Other colors, close colors, but not that particular red."

"You know," Bradley mused, "a few years ago I would have filed a call like this under 'prankster.'"

"Call the medical examiner," Saffron commanded.

Bradley went on as if he hadn't heard her, "But now, after so many of your tips have panned out over the years, I find myself ready to dial the medical examiner."

"Call her," Saffron said again, "I think this is poisoning."

"Okay. Also, why do you sound like you're calling from the bathtub?"

"I am calling from the bathtub," she snapped.

"Oookay," Bradley said. She could tell he was trying hard not to say more.

"You saw the news today, then?" Saffron demanded.

"Well, sure, everybody saw that."

"I'm not involved with Zayne Grayson!" Saffron blurted.

"Hey, nobody's judging."

"I'm not. And if you have nothing better to do than to peruse the celebrity gossip sites, then why don't you come out here and clear off all the photographers who are trespassing on my private property?"

At this he balked. Bradley was notorious for not liking to go out of his way to do his job, "Can't. I've got to call Arlene, the medical examiner."

Saffron hung up half annoyed and half amused. Bradley always seemed to have that effect.

"I can't stay in here all day," she said, checking her watch. She was supposed to be on set in under two hours, and she still had all her chicken chores to do.

Suddenly, she imagined her image smeared across the magazines: boots unlaced, smudges on her face, hair adorned with a stray feather or two, holding handfuls of eggs. The media would have a heyday.

She was grateful to see, hanging on the back of the bathroom door, the new dress the Empress had brought over. She slipped into it, grateful for its soft and comfortable fit. She took a look at her hair. It was nearly always a little wild, so it didn't need too much attention.

Now, how was she going to get out of here without being seen?

She opened the bathroom door. The sound of feet and voices still echoed outside. There would be no going through the front door.

She tiptoed down the hall and stood at an angle to the open guest bedroom door. Through it, she could see out the windows onto the lanai. There were still photographers everywhere. Since they couldn't shoot Saffron, they seemed to be focused on the very angry rooster that was clucking on the lanai railing.

The next events happened very quickly and very loudly. There was a general rumble of disturbance in the group on the lanai, then a few shouts of genuine alarm.

Saffron raced down the hallway and looked out the front windows just in time to see her donkey, Jasper, headed at full tilt for the group on the lanai.

There was scrambling and scattering and swearing from outside.

Jasper didn't stop as he neared the house, simply kicked up his heels and launched over the railing of the lanai to land squarely between the front windows and the now-terrified paparazzi. He snorted and stomped, dancing toward them threateningly. Saffron had never seen him act like this. He was, usually, a true marshmallow.

Curry joined in, too. Flapping and raking the air with his long talons, he aimed for the cameras.

The photographers took off for their cars. They slammed doors, trailing camera straps and microphone cords, and left behind them a cloud of dust as they tore down the long drive-way, Jasper and Curry in hot pursuit.

Saffron couldn't stop giggling. Jasper was kicking and braying like a demon, Curry crowing and flapping like a whirlwind.

Carefully, she glanced around and peered out onto the lanai. How had Jasper gotten out? Last night he had been solidly locked in his stall in the barn.

Glancing toward it, she saw what had happened. Mano and Slate stood beside the open barn door, leaning on each other for support as they guffawed at the sight of the scrambling paparazzi and the guard donkey.

When Jasper was sure the intruders were gone, he gave a final, angry snort and stomped both of his front feet with finality. Curry strutted back and forth at the end of the driveway like a tin soldier.

Slate and Mano gave Saffron a friendly wave. Though her intent had been to keep them away, she was awfully glad she had texted them.

When Bradley called later, Saffron was not surprised to hear that the medical examiner had found high levels of lead in Shar's body.

"Great," Saffron said, "Now we can try to figure out who might have been tampering with Shar's makeup."

Bradley's voice was harsh, "Not great."

"Not great?"

"No. The examiner wanted to know how I thought to check for lead, and I told her. Now I've got to question you."

"Question me?"

"Yes. Think about it. You were the first person on the scene AND you knew to check for lead poisoning. You're not good at looking innocent."

"But I am innocent."

"Then try harder to look that way when I interview you in an hour."

The Maika'i police station was a strange take on a law enforcement headquarters. There was one secretary—Harriet —that sat in the big entry room and answered the phone, a few cells in the back and upstairs, and a couple offices, along with a break room.

The uniqueness came from the decor. Because Harriet didn't have a lot of actual crime to keep her busy, she made art out of seashells. Hawaii gave her unlimited materials, and her job gave her unlimited time. She spent that time encrusting everything: the light switches, the file cabinets, the staplers, with seashells. She also made seashell mosaic pictures of seagulls and seascapes. The result was a little dizzying.

Bradley's office hadn't escaped Harriet's artistry. Saffron scraped her arm on some hairy triton shells at the edge of Bradley's desk.

"Sorry," he mumbled, "they get me, too."

The interview was perfunctory. He asked her her whereabouts, her knowledge of the victim, how she knew about the lead.

"I've only seen that color a couple of times before," Saffron said.

Bradley bit the end of a pencil encrusted with tiny beige shells, "What is it with you and colors?" he asked, "I mean, you're always talking about them."

Saffron shrugged, "I guess I'm just more sensitive to them than other people are," she admitted. She'd known for a long time that she could see more colors than other people could, but it was still a new concept for most people.

"More sensitive?"

"Yeah, it's like, you know, how dogs can hear dog whistles, but we can't because our ears don't pick up that frequency? I guess it's something like that, but with my eyes. Most people think there are fewer colors than I do."

"That's an interesting superpower," Bradley mused.

"An inconvenient one sometimes," she admitted.

"I'm sure."

"But useful in cases like this one," she said.

Bradley looked at her, his square face open and sincere, "I know you didn't have anything to do with this lady's death."

"Thanks," Saffron said. There were perks of living in a small town.

"But if she was poisoned, then we gotta open an investigation, and there's a chance other agencies might get involved, and I can't promise they won't see the facts differently than I do."

The thought made Saffron shiver.

"I can hold the investigation up in paperwork for a few days," he said, "and it won't get any attention until I file it, but, Saffron, if you have any ideas about who might be responsible, let's you and me get them checked out and see if we can nab someone before everybody else comes in and starts askin' questions."

That seemed like a very wise course of action to Saffron. As she stood, Bradley stood, too, and put on his hat.

"You heading down to the set?" he asked.

Saffron nodded. She had a line in today's script.

"Me, too. They've moved the set, you know, and they're shooting in the middle of town the next few days, so I've got to reroute traffic to the side streets."

"I'm glad you'll be nearby," Saffron said.

"You let me know if you see anything suspicious."

Chapter Nine

The scenes at Shell Beach had all been shot. The story was moving on to the scenes in town, and Holoholo Street had been transformed into a strangely artificial version of itself. The little shops along the street had been given a facelift, with new, temporary signs and more trendy fashions in the windows. Cameras coasted down the middle of the street and boom microphones hovered over the boardwalk like hungry birds. A production assistant shooed a little flock of feral chickens off the boardwalk into the bushes beside the shops.

They'll be back, Saffron thought. Feral chickens were ubiquitous in Hawaii.

She could see a knot of people in front of the Tropical Adventures Travel Agency building. At its center, Elyse and Zayne were shooting a scene. Saffron wondered if he knew how much trouble their encounter on the beach yesterday had caused her.

One end of the street had been blocked by the stars' trailers. The other by the makeup trailer, the costume trailer, and the catering trucks.

Saffron's friends and neighbors mingled at the edges, watching for a glimpse of any star. Saffron herself was apparently famous enough, because when they saw her, they rushed forward to get the scoop.

"Oh! Saffron, how exciting! You've been swept up by Zayne Grayson!" Saffron's friend Fumi, who ran a kitchen gadget store, was nearly crying with excitement.

Saffron shook her head, "Don't believe everything you read."

"I hope not," another voice from behind the crowd drew Saffron's attention. The townspeople quieted and parted, making way for Nik to stride forward.

His usually easy posture was tight, and his shoulders were more square than Saffron had ever seen them. He was steeling himself for bad news.

"Nik!" she rushed forward, sliding her arms around him, but he didn't relax. Saffron stepped back awkwardly, suddenly very aware of the crowd gathered around them.

"Can we talk?" he asked gruffly.

Saffron caught his hand and led him to the first private place she saw: Elyse's trailer. She knocked lightly, but Elyse was over on the boardwalk, so she knew the trailer would be available.

"C'mon, in here," she said, pulling him inside.

Nik paused at the doorway, not because he was unsure about using someone else's trailer, but because he was amazed at the opulence inside.

"This is epic," he said, "it's nicer than my house."

"Mine, too," Saffron grinned.

He tensed again, looking away from her.

"Nik!" she tugged at his arm, "Come on! You know that I'm not involved with Zayne."

"You're apparently on a first-name basis with him," Nik said petulantly.

"Nik! You can't believe that story!"

"Why not?"

"Zayne's not interested in me. Look at me! I'm not his type."

"You're beautiful. Kind. Intelligent. Funny. Saffron, you're everybody's type."

How could Nik infuriate her and melt her heart with the same sentence? She took his other hand in hers, holding tight when he tried to pull away.

"I've had two conversations with him, that's all."

"It took me a lot less than that to fall for you," Nik said, "And I saw the pictures, Saffron."

"The pictures are . . ." she tried to think of the right word, "misleading. There was this photographer, and I don't know, he got the angle wrong or something. You know how those guys are, they're after a story, even if there's not really a story."

Nik squeezed her hands, "I believe you, and I know you'd tell me the truth, but it's, you know, it's just got me thinking is all."

Saffron felt his next words coming like a low pressure system before a storm. They seemed to suck all the air out of the room, "Saffron, I'm not sure we're . . . working."

"Nik! I'm telling you, there's nothing going on—"

His eyes searched her face, and his jaw set. She'd never seen him so upset, "It's not about that. I'm just," his voice broke, "I've known for a while, and I've been trying to decide if I was right or not, and when I saw those photos of you with Zayne, I knew—" he stopped her before she could protest further, "not because of what I saw, but because of what I felt. I didn't feel angry. I didn't feel sad. I felt relieved, Saffron, because I thought maybe you had finally found someone who deserves you."

"Nik!"

"No, listen, you're amazing."

Saffron didn't feel amazing. She felt frantic, like another thing she loved was washing out with the tide and the pull of the ocean was too strong for her to hold on to it.

"You're amazing, and you're ready for all this real stuff in your life, like marriage, and maybe kids—"

"What? I've never—"

"You don't have to say anything. I saw you taking care of those Tucker kids a couple months ago. You were a natural at it. I can see it—you're going to want that someday, and I'm not sure I will."

"We don't need to decide that now," Saffron said, fear rising in her stomach.

"Yeah," Nik said, "yeah we do. Because I'm going on this surfing circuit, and I don't want you waiting around here for me. I don't want you spending every night in the bungalow. I want you to go to hukilaus and parties and dance with the best guys there. I want you to have someone who is as excited about your egg farm as you are, who isn't going to be running off chasing that perfect curl or that epic wave. Maybe it's because of my childhood, or maybe it's surfing, or maybe it's just who I am, but I'm going to disappear sometimes, and I'm going to live out of my station wagon sometimes, and I'm going to sleep on the beach and eat flying fish out of a truck sometimes, and I'm not going to think about calling or coming home until days have passed. I've known that about myself for a long time. I have twenty-three dollars in my bank account, and that's the most I've had for like two years. I get it, and I spend it, and I work to make some more, and I spend that. Don't you see? I'm just not cut out for a real, grown-up life."

Saffron didn't feel the tears on her cheeks until she saw the tears running down his. He was serious. He meant this.

"Maybe it's not Zayne," he said, "but someone's going to come along who's going to share your dreams and help you build them. Maybe," he put a hand under her chin and tipped her face up toward his, "Maybe it's Keahi."

The name was like a hot blade across her heart.

Nik kept talking, "Maybe you'll want to go to Boston and see if you can work things out with him. I know he really loves you, Saffron."

She let go of his hand and stepped back, bumping into the granite countertop in the kitchen area of the trailer, "Don't count on it," she said bitterly.

"Sure," Nik tried to sound cheerful, "you don't know, it could still work out with him," he was trying to make it better, but Saffron's shoulders shook more with every word.

Finally, she blurted out the sentence that had been running underneath her thoughts ever since she'd found out: "He's getting married."

Nik breathed out a big gust, as if he'd been punched in the stomach, "What? Aw, bummer, Saffron, I'm sorry."

"It's fine," she said, "I've been over him for a long time."

The look Nik gave her said they both knew that wasn't true. She loved Nik for knowing that. Silence stretched between them.

It was in that moment of quiet that Saffron heard it—a tiny sound, like the rustle of an autumn leaf in a winter tree, scuffing against the bare bark. She froze.

"Hello?" she called out.

From the front of the trailer, where the door stood open to the bedroom, a voice called back, "Hello!"

Saffron flinched as the wispy-haired man with the rusty stubble on his chin and the yellow-tinted glasses stepped through the doorway. He had been in the trailer the whole time, had probably heard Nik breaking up with her. Saffron's cheeks burned.

"I'm sorry," the man said, "by the time I realized you were

here, it was far too late to interrupt and let you know I was, too."

Saffron closed her eyes and shook her head, "It's my fault," she said, her stomach churning, "I shouldn't have come in here. I thought it would be a short conversation."

Nik was standing squarely between the small man and Saffron, "I'm sorry," he said, "who are you?"

"I'm Kirk Marshall," the man did not offer a hand, instead, he used both to grip the handle of his briefcase, "Ms. Avery's, er, accountant."

Saffron felt a little rush of pride that she'd guessed correctly about his profession.

"And you just listened to our whole conversation without saying anything?" Nik was getting belligerent.

Saffron didn't need him getting into a brawl with the scrawny accountant. She stepped forward, laid a hand on his arm, and pulled him toward the door, "We were just going."

The compassion in the little man's eyes led Saffron to believe that he had known some pain himself.

"I'm happy to step out," he said, "if you need a few more moments to talk."

Saffron looked at Nik as she spoke, "I don't think there's really anything left to say."

———

SAFFRON'S SCENE that afternoon had Gwen Thistledown running into Elyse and Zayne at a gift shop and asking about Adam's character, who she had seen Elyse with before. It was meant to be an awkward confrontation, and standing across from Zayne, who had obviously seen the article, infused the air with just the right amount of discomfort.

"Brilliant! Brilliant!" Blum called from the sidelines, "that's a wrap! Take ten minutes, everybody!"

Saffron had loved being Gwen for a few moments. Stepping into her fictional character had allowed her to leave behind the mess that was her real life for the duration of the scene.

That dropped away as soon as Blum wrapped the scene. She was back to being plain old Saffron, standing in front of two of the world's biggest stars.

"Well," Elyse said, her voice harsh, "I guess the two of you would probably like some time alone," she turned toward her trailer.

"Wait!" Saffron said, "No, we don't. Do we?" she looked pleadingly at Zayne.

"Of course not," his tone was impatient as he double-stepped to catch up with Elyse. Saffron trailed along a few paces behind them, not sure if the conversation still included her.

Adam swooped in from the edge of the set, too, falling into step with Elyse on the other side, "You want to come to my trailer for a snack? I've got some prime stuff in there from lunch."

"I'm not hungry," Elyse said, outpacing both men as she strode to her trailer, climbed in, and, as well as she could with an aluminum door, slammed it.

"What's with her?" Adam shrugged.

"It's been a long shoot," Zayne said, "and she's under a lot of pressure from Blum. I heard him trying to convince her to do his next film."

"Tough problem to have: world's most popular director wants you in his movie."

"Yeah, well," Zayne turned around abruptly and nearly ran into Saffron. His scowl made her take two steps backward, "Can I help you with something?"

Something inside Saffron snapped. She didn't care who he was, he had no right to talk to her like that. Everyone else around her may have thought he was royalty, but she knew he was just a regular guy with a lot of extra luck.

"Yes," she said, raising her chin, "you can. You can hunt down that Rossi character and set him straight about us."

Zayne's eyebrows rose, "Excuse me?"

"His little story has created unnecessary havoc in my life all day. You find him and have him take it back."

"Take it back?" Zayne exchanged a look with Adam, whose smirk told Saffron she was being unreasonable, but she didn't care. Someone should be held responsible for the chaos that had been introduced into her life and into her relationship with Nik.

"That's right. They told the lie, they can tell the truth and set the record straight."

"That's not how it works," Zayne said. For a moment, she thought she saw a glimmer of true regret in his eyes.

"How does it work, then?"

"Listen, Saffron, here's how it works. We ignore them. Go on, live your life, do your thing. They'll eventually forget about you and move on. You fight with them, it just gets a whole lot worse."

"How could it get any worse?" Saffron fumed.

The men exchanged another look, a knowing one, and Adam said, "Oh, believe me, it can get a lot worse."

Chapter Ten

Looking through the celebrity magazines late that night with a bowl of ice cream and Holly for company, Saffron saw what they had been talking about. Adam Sullivan was, right now, embroiled in a battle over his reaction to a photographer who had spread lies about him. He'd gone after the man in court and the story had spread further than it ever would have if he'd simply left it alone.

"It must be awful," Holly said, "to live so publicly."

"From my vast experience," Saffron said, taking a bite of sweet chocolate macadamia nut ice cream, "it is."

She ran a finger over the glossy photo of Adam in the magazine. He was dressed in a suit, striding angrily out of the courtroom, where he apparently stopped to throw his cup of soda all over a waiting photographer. There were pictures of the spraying soda, the ice cubes flying through the air, the photographer cowering. That probably hadn't helped Adam's image either.

From what Saffron could tell, image was everything. Some celebrities were branded by their addictions or their affairs, some by their charity work or their children. None of them were presented by these magazines as whole people, with good days and bad days, strengths and weaknesses. They were boiled down to one image, which the tabloids flashed at the audiences over and over and over until the readers forgot that they were looking at human beings.

Saffron had bookmarked the pages with the actors she was working with, and she flipped through them now.

Ace Carnation was on a few pages. Mostly in the background of other people's shots. Rarely was he the sole subject of the photo.

Zayne, of course, was featured several times in each magazine. Here he was leaving a restaurant, here he was at the premier of his last film, here he was at a charity event for a children's hospital.

Always smiling. Always alone.

Then there was Adam. Angry one moment, friendly the next. Seen fairly often with female co-stars at social events, which indicated that he spent some time on his romantic life. Saffron had seen evidence of that on the set as he'd tried to build something with Elyse.

And Elyse herself. She was glamour personified. The

tabloids loved her. She was featured in red-carpet photos as well as articles about style and articles about staying youthful. Only one article tried to cast her in a negative light, claiming she was putting on pounds, but Saffron took another bite of ice cream and turned the page. The photo of the elegant star certainly didn't convince her of their claim.

Nik had been right. Elyse never looked tired, never seemed out-of-sorts. She was perpetually gentle and smiling, whether they photographed her leaving the spa or finishing a 5K race.

Saffron flipped back to the photos and held two of them side-by-side. She must have made a sound that revealed her puzzlement, because Holly looked up and said, "What is it?"

Saffron squinted at the photos. In one, Elyse was wearing a midnight blue evening gown and standing in front of a limousine. In the other, she was wearing a white tee shirt, blue jeans, and sitting astride a horse. Her smile was identical in both, but something was different about the two photos. Saffron pointed to the star's eyes.

"Do her eyes look different colors to you?"

Holly scooted across the futon and peered at the photos, "Greenish-gray. And," looking at the other one, "also greenish-gray."

Saffron waved a hand impatiently, sure of what she was seeing, "Yes, yes, I know. They're both greenish-gray. But one," she pointed to Elyse on the horse, "is lovat green and the other," she pointed to Elyse by the limo, "is more sage green."

"Are those even real colors?" Holly asked.

"Sure. Sage is a little more silvery gray, while lovat has a slightly bluish tinge to the gray in the green."

Holly did what nearly every person in Saffron's life did at one point or another: she squinted at the photos and leaned forward to study them very closely, then shook her head, "They look the same to me."

But the more Saffron studied them, the more she saw

it, "No, I'm sure they're slightly different. But why?" Eye color was something Saffron had found particularly consistent most of the time. It was usually unique enough that she sometimes used it to identify different people in a crowd.

The thought came to her, and she wondered if it were simply because she'd been thinking of it lately. She said it out loud, "Could it be drugs? Or a toxin of some sort? I know those can dilate the pupils, maybe they can cause the iris to appear different colors?"

"You think Elyse Avery is on drugs?" Holly was incredulous. She flipped through her magazine, "None of these say anything about that. No hint of rehab or crazy outbursts or anything."

"I don't know. But there's definitely a difference in her eye color," Saffron pulled out a few more photos and noticed it in several of them. Sometimes Elyse had the slightly bluer eyes, sometimes the slightly more silver. "Of course," she mused, it could be that the ink these are printed with is slightly different. Or the lighting."

To Holly's credit, she didn't say, *Or you could just be crazy*. But Saffron suspected by her new friend's sideways glance that she might be thinking exactly that.

Saffron realized she didn't know enough about poisons. If Elyse had access to some kind of toxin, would that cause the changes in eye color Saffron was noticing? And was she another victim, or had Elyse been involved in Shar's death?

A noise outside the open window made Saffron look up. Holly didn't seem to have noticed. Not wanting to concern her friend, Saffron slid the magazines off her lap and went through the kitchen to the back door.

Outside, the island evening rested warm and welcoming. Saffron stepped out onto the lanai, feeling the gathering dew on the boards beneath her bare feet. This side of the house was dark, the only light coming from the windows of the cottages across the wide lawn.

Voices.

Saffron froze, easing the screen door closed behind her. Men's voices. Glad she was barefoot, Saffron pressed into the shadow of the roof and slipped down to the back edge of the house.

There, off the lanai, in the deep shade of a hibiscus tree, stood two figures. The sound of their voices reached Saffron, and she knew immediately who one of them was.

"Listen, I'm telling you, the real money is in shots of Elyse. People are getting tired of talking about Zayne," the sneer in the words, the way he dropped the 'r's, the 'aw' sound in the middle of talk . . . all added up to the strong New York accent of Ace Carnation.

"I made really good money for those beach shots," the other voice was high, delicate, with the lilt of Italian somewhere behind the syllables. Saffron guessed this was the illusive Rossi.

"Not half the money you'll make if you can get something on Elyse."

"Get something? What something? The woman is perfection. She's never out of sorts, never involved in scandal, never has a single eyelash out of place."

"Too perfect," Ace spat, "which tells me there's a story there. You need to dig harder. Did you get any shots of Adam leaving her cottage tonight?"

What? Adam had been in Elyse's cottage? Saffron had missed that.

"No, I—" Rossi's tone was chagrined, "I didn't make it in time. All was quiet here when I arrived."

"Tell me you at least got her in the car with the makeup guy?"

Saffron blinked, Elyse had also been talking to Roman?

"No. Missed that, too."

"How about the accountant?"

"He's about as interesting on film as peeling paint," Saffron had to agree with that. Kirk had a strange, colorless quality that wouldn't read well in a glossy magazine spread.

"What have you been doing then?"

"I told you. I think something's up with Zayne. I've been trying to figure out what so I can break the story."

Ace swore, "Listen, just because you've made some money on him—"

"No, listen, he's looking at houses around here. I think he might be going to buy one."

This was news to Saffron. She leaned a little further out, trying to catch every word.

"What do we care about his real estate decisions?" Ace said, "You're obsessed with him. You just can't see the big picture. You're pigeonholing yourself. Pretty soon the press will only come to you for pictures of him, and you'll miss out on all the other revenue you could be making from other shots."

"What do you care?" Rossi's tone was belligerent.

"I care because you owe me money, and I owe other people money. You don't pay me, I don't pay them, my legs get broken."

A long silence settled across the yard. The distant whoosh of the ocean reached them. It sounded, in the dark, like gentle breathing.

Ace finally spoke again, "Do you at least have any more recordings of the egg farmer for me?"

Saffron's breath caught. Had Rossi been listening in on her conversations?

"Yeah, but you're not going to like this one."

"What do you mean?"

"The last one got you all that praise from Blum for adding that great scene into the script. But I'm afraid that train has left the station. You're not going to be getting anything else to further your writing career from the egg farmer and the surfer." There was a click, and Saffron recognized it as some kind of device being turned on. Her own voice filled the night.

"The pictures are . . . misleading . . ." Saffron knew exactly when she had said that, and as Nik's voice filled the night, she knew exactly what was coming next.

"Saffron, I'm not sure we're . . . working."

It didn't hurt any less to hear it for the second time.

"Ouch," Ace said. There was a strange satisfaction in his voice.

"I know. Poor kid," Rossi seemed genuinely sorry for Saffron. If, that was, he was capable of any genuine feelings. "Still, it'll be a great follow-up to the story about her and Zayne: *Star's new flame breaks up with surfer boyfriend.*"

Saffron gritted her teeth.

Rossi went on, "And a great lead-up to his buying real estate here: *Star buys estate in paradise to be near new love interest.*"

"That's not all," Ace said grimly, "I can use it, too."

"You going to write it into the script?"

"Sure. That line's gold: we're not working. Elyse's character can use it in the break-up scene with Adam. It's better than the line they have now."

Saffron's stomach twisted. The movie really was in parallel to her real life. Ace was injecting her experiences into the script.

Rossi cleared his throat, "Why you want to be a writer, anyway?" he asked, "You've been putting all this effort into impressing Blum with your additions to the script, but why? When you're already an established actor?"

"Established, maybe, A-list, never. As an actor, Ross, I'll always be second-rate. But as a writer, maybe I can make a name for myself and rise to the top." Ace sniffed and shifted, his steps making shushing sounds in the foliage, "Besides, writers don't have to worry about paparazzi scum tracking their every move."

Saffron was interested to hear how Rossi responded to the insult, but she didn't get the chance. Out of the darkness exploded a braying, bucking Jasper.

"What the—" Ace cried, cut off by Curry's crow of anger. Both animals had been roaming since earlier, and Saffron pressed back into the shadows as Ace and Rossi ran off toward the safety of Ace's cottage.

"I dropped the recorder," Rossi cried.

"Leave it. We'll get it in the morning, when these demons are locked up," Ace's tone was no longer cool and detached. He was running for his life now.

Once the cottage door slammed and the two men stopped peering out the front window, Saffron slipped down off the lanai and found the recorder in the tall grass by the hibiscus tree. She carried it back inside.

Holly looked up as she came in from the kitchen, "Getting a midnight snack?"

"Not exactly," Saffron held up the recorder and explained to Holly what she had heard.

"What? Are you kidding? They've been listening in on you?"

"Apparently," Saffron wasn't about to play any of the conversation, even for Holly.

"I think that's illegal."

"Probably."

Holly's eyebrows drew together. She flipped her tiger-striped hair and reached up for Saffron's hand, "Saf, how are you doing? I mean, about Nik?"

Saffron wanted to cry. She had that trembly, empty feeling in the pit of her stomach, but she was out of tears and she was out of words. She sunk onto the futon and shook her head.

SAFFRON WAS UP LONG before dawn the next day. It was Tuesday, and the locals would be lining up in their cars for the Tuesday Egg Line, where Saffron stood at the top of her driveway and exchanged cartons of eggs for payment. It was convenient for the customers, efficient for Saffron, and she looked forward to it every week. This week, she was sure, she'd have lots of questions about the movie set to answer, and maybe a few about Zayne Grayson, too.

She made her way down to the egg house in the cool, damp dark of the early morning. Jasper was standing guard near the front doors, and she stopped to give him a good scratch.

"Thanks for your help, buddy," she said, "you're a good guard donkey."

Jasper let out a happy grunt.

Curry, following at Saffron's heels, bawked. She leaned down and scratched his chest, too, "And you," she said, "you make a good team."

"You're probably hungry, huh?" she asked the donkey. She led him to the barn and opened his stall door. He trotted inside.

"I'm gonna keep you in here this morning," she said, "with all the cars coming for the egg line." Though she often had him pull the little egg cart to the top of the driveway and stand while she handed out the eggs, she thought today the customers might be a bit too chatty. Sometimes, when customers dawdled, Jasper was too social. He'd been known to stick his head in an open car window to say hello if a customer tarried too long.

She gave him a big scoop of grain, and he didn't seem to mind staying behind as she went to take care of the hens.

Her girls greeted her with a cacophony of chortles and

clucks. The egg house had a cozy feel, with its bright yellow lights and the warmth from the hens. A soft breeze blew in the wire-covered windows and somehow everything else happening in Saffron's life seemed a distant memory.

Tikka, Saffron's first friend on the farm, called out a three-note greeting that the hens seemed to reserve for Saffron. In response, Saffron tossed a handful of scratch grains into Tikka's pen.

The fluffy Salmon Faverolles that had come to live with Saffron last Christmas bounced over to snatch up their favorite bits: the cracked corn.

The other hens in the other pens set up a racket for treats of their own, and Saffron spent the next few minutes walking up and down the aisle, tossing scratch into each pen and chatting with her girls.

"Ahhh, Sunshine, I see you're coming out of your molt nicely. Look at those glossy new feathers! And Cleo, I didn't think it was possible for you to get any fluffier, but you've done it!" She stopped at the last pen, the one set up for Cupcake and her chicks.

"Cupcake, how are you doing after losing one of your brood?" Saffron had been worried that Cupcake would take Duchess' absence hard, but in truth, the other two kadaknath chicks seemed to be keeping the mother hen busy enough that she hadn't noticed. They were, right now, playing a game of keep-away with a bug. Cupcake looked on indulgently.

Saffron loved the easy pace of her morning egg gathering. This week, in particular, she noticed the quiet rhythm of her regular days. After the bustle of the set, people yelling every few moments, herding her here or there, or ordering her to turn this way or that way, the egg house, its calm inhabitants, and her own company felt right and peaceful.

She stood in the work area at the front of the egg house and cranked the conveyor belts that carried the eggs from the roll-out nest boxes to her. Plucking them from the belt like oversized grapes, she put each carefully in the long, narrow channel of brushes that was the egg washer.

On the other end of the washer, the eggs rolled out under an air dryer into a clean, flat bin. She picked them from there and put them in cartons, organizing them, of course, by color.

When she'd gathered them all, she stacked them on her egg cart and hauled them up to the house, where she collected the rest of the week's eggs from the avocado-green refrigerator on the lanai. She wheeled the cart to the top of the driveway just as the sun began to touch the sky beyond the palm trees.

In the beginning, it was like any other egg Tuesday. Her earliest customers showed up right on time, and a steady stream of cars was soon gliding past.

It was about half an hour in that Saffron began to notice strange additions.

People were walking up the beach in groups of two or ten, ogling the line of cars, the house, and Saffron herself. They were not locals, so the chance they were there for eggs was slim. She began to get an uneasy feeling.

More people came—this time zooming past the egg line cars on the other side of the driveway, causing blockages or veering out off the driveway onto the lawn to get around oncoming cars. They parked in front of Saffron's house and got out.

Some of them had expensive cameras and the distinctive dismissal of personal space that characterized the paparazzi. Some, though, were obviously tourists.

They spread out over the farm. One group had the nerve to approach Saffron and shout, "Excuse me? Where is Zayne Grayson staying? Are you his new flame? Is he here?"

Someone had leaked that the stars were staying here. Saffron would bet that someone was Ace Carnation.

Chapter Eleven

Her farm was a disaster. Zayne and Elyse had been forced to duck into the back of Saffron's Thunderbird and she'd driven them through scores of people and finally dropped them off at the set on Holoholo Street. The crowd there had grown exponentially, too. It seemed that the rest of the island had finally realized something big was happening in Maika'i.

Nosing the Thunderbird through the crowds and into the parking lot set aside for the movie traffic, Saffron felt relieved when she deposited Elyse and Zayne safely. She caught sight of Bradley as she made her way past the catering table.

"Anything new?" she asked.

He shook his head, taking a bite of a large chocolate pastry, "Nothing yet. I'm here to clear the trailer and let the assistant makeup artist back in. You got anything for me?"

"Not yet," Saffron swallowed hard, thinking of the investigation opening and the questions she'd have to field if she didn't come up with a suspect.

She walked with Bradley to the makeup trailer, but they found the steps blocked by an unlikely trio: Bernie, owner of the pet shop, Doc Morgan, the town's handsome new veterinarian, and Echo.

"Oh, no," the words slipped out as Saffron saw Echo. The big, beautiful bird lay limp in Bernie's hands. Doc Morgan was peering closely at Echo's eyelids and listening with a stethoscope to her chest. "What's wrong?"

"Don't know," Bernie shrugged. His face was haggard, "I found her this way this morning when I came to get her for the scene."

Saffron ran two fingers over the smooth curve of Echo's head. The bird opened one eye and looked at her. "Get out of here!" Echo choked.

Bernie rallied, "She's not gone yet! What can you do, Doc?"

Doc Morgan shook his head sadly, "I don't know. We can get her back to the office and start her on some fluids, but unless I know what happened, I won't know how to treat her."

Saffron knew. She spoke up, "Lead."

"I'm sorry?"

"Would lead hurt a bird?"

"Sure, it's highly toxic to them."

Bernie jumped in, "But scarlet macaws eat toxic plants in the wild and they survive by eating clay that binds with the toxins and rids the birds of them."

"That's right," Saffron remembered Bernie telling her this before, "If this is lead poisoning, is there anything you can use to get it out?"

Doc Morgan nodded, "There are three options for treating heavy metal toxicosis in birds—a type of calcium, an acid called DMSA, or D-penicillamine. They can work like the clay —bind with the lead to flush it out of the bird before any more is absorbed."

"Good!" Saffron urged, "Do that!"

Doc Morgan looked at her quizzically, "But what makes you so sure it's lead poisoning?"

Saffron didn't have time to go into her visual acuity just now. She looked pleadingly at Bradley.

"Just trust her," he said, "it's lead."

As the men bustled off to the veterinarian's office with Echo, Saffron and Bradley entered the trailer.

"How did she get ahold of it?" Bradley asked, his gaze pointed toward Echo's cage.

Saffron was peering at the counter, "The same way Shar did. In the air."

"What? I thought you said it was in her makeup."

"It was," Saffron pointed to the white counter, then to the mirror, "Look closely."

Bradley did, then shook his head, "Come on, Saffron. Don't play around. You know I can't see it. Just tell me what you're seeing."

"Dots," she said, "tiny red specks all over in here."

"And they're this color you said, this minimum?"

"Minium," she corrected, "and yes. The more I look, the more I see: on the lights, on the floor. Specks everywhere, like a minium bomb went off in here. I think the lead was airborne. I think Shar and Echo breathed it in. Call the medical examiner and see if that's possible, and if that would hurt them."

Bradley shrugged and dialed a number on his cell phone. Saffron used hers to snap some zoomed-in photos of the specks. She inspected the open makeup cases and was surprised to see no powder that matched the color. There were plenty of reds, but none that were an exact match.

When Bradley hung up, he looked discouraged.

"What?" Saffron pressed, "Am I wrong? Would airborne minium not hurt someone?"

"No, no," Bradley interrupted, "You're absolutely right.

The examiner says that a large amount of it, inhaled at once, could cause acute toxicity like what killed Shar."

"Why do you look so down then?"

"Because you're not making it any easier for them not to suspect you. The medical examiner says she's going to open the investigation herself if I don't get that paperwork in."

Saffron looked around, "Just give me a couple more days. Now that I know how it happened, I just need to figure out the why and the who."

"Well make it snappy, or the who's gonna be you," Bradley growled.

"I've got one idea," she said, "he's got motive and means, I just don't know about opportunity. I can't find anything that ties him directly to this place at the time of the murder."

"Sounds like a lead, anyway."

"C'mon," Saffron said, "he's working out of the costume trailer for now."

———

ROMAN WAS HARRIED and impatient with their questions. Saffron noticed a tremor in the artist's hands that revealed his discomfort with their presence. He nearly poked one of the background characters' eyes out trying to apply some eye shadow.

"I have no idea what you're talking about. I've never heard of mini—whatever."

"But you were familiar with Shar's makeup kit, I assume?" Saffron asked.

"Of course."

"And did you notice a particular shade of red blush inside?"

"Girl, she had a dozen shades of red. Liked the bold look, you know? I warned her about it five years ago."

"Warned her about lead?"

"No, warned her about makeup that was far too young for her. She didn't seem to care, just kept right on with the most garish stuff she could find."

"And where did she get her makeup?"

"Regular suppliers. Not the grocery store," Roman shot Saffron a scathing look, "that's for sure."

"I didn't see this exact color in her kit," Saffron said.

"Not her kit in the trailer. That's for clients. Her personal kit was probably in her purse, or at her hotel."

Saffron exchanged a look with Bradley.

"Thank you," she said, "we may be back with more questions."

"You'd better be back in an hour with your face ready," Roman snapped, "you're on set at noon."

THE MORGUE in the hospital was not a new place for Saffron, but this was the first time she'd visited it with an official escort. Bradley detained the medical examiner, who kept shooting wary glances at Saffron, while Saffron, wearing gloves and a mask, retrieved Shar's kit from her purse in the big plastic bag of her belongings. Saffron tried not to look at the clothes there, or the leopard-print high heels that Shar would never wear again. She tried not to notice the makeup brushes that had been in Shar's pockets. The artist would never wield them again.

When she laid the makeup bag on the steel table in the center of the room, the medical examiner, whose nametag read *Arlene Winn*, and Bradley, both masked and gloved, gathered around.

Saffron was not surprised to see the red dust on the bag,

and in one of the little metal wells inside. She nodded at Bradley.

"Which one?" he asked.

Saffron pointed it out for him. She was keenly aware of Arlene's gaze. The woman had slick black hair, pulled into a tight bun at the back of her head, and sharp gray eyes.

"Officer Bradley here tells me you have . . . exceptional color vision?"

"That's right," Saffron said, "Can you see the difference between this one, this orangey red, and the stuff under it?"

She could tell that the woman could not. "Well, do a chemical analysis, and that will give you the same results," Saffron said.

"Could you, er, wait outside there?" the woman gestured to the door.

Saffron could see that she was still suspicious. She obliged, stripping off her clingy gloves and mask and depositing them in the biohazard bin near the door as she left.

She didn't have to wonder what the medical examiner was saying to Bradley. She would be urging him to arrest Saffron before she made a run for it.

Saffron wandered down the hall. It was a nice hospital, bright and airy and full of natural wood and glass. She'd been here a few times since arriving in Maika'i, both as a visitor and as a patient. Passing by a conference room, Saffron stopped to admire a photograph of Shell Beach.

She didn't mean to overhear, but the conversation happening in the conference room was loud and heated.

"You tell me what we can do then?"

"We don't have a choice. We're going to have to shut down surgery services. It's far too expensive to keep bringing these doctors up from Honolulu."

"We need a surgeon here!"

"I know that. We've looked. The fact is that decent

surgeons can work anywhere, and they're not interested in our little town, or the much smaller salary we can offer them. Big hospitals are always going to win."

"If we shut down the surgery unit, it means the people of Maika'i are out of luck if they get an appendicitis, or a ruptured gall bladder—we can't even deliver babies without a surgery safety net."

The first voice was subdued, "I realize that. There just isn't another option."

Saffron's heart was pounding. This was terrible. Maika'i needed all the medical services it could get. She couldn't stop herself. Hating every word, she popped her head around the doorway and blurted, "I'm sorry. I overheard you. Have you, you know, have you asked anyone local? I mean, who grew up locally? I mean, specifically, have you asked Keahi Kekoa?"

She hated saying it, hated thinking of him coming back to Maika'i as a newlywed, but it was the right thing to do.

Three hospital administrators were in the room—two men Saffron had met before and one woman she didn't recognize who said, "Excuse me, who are you?"

"This is Saffron Skye, our local egg farmer and event planner," explained Herb Grover, the Director of Services.

Makani Kawai, the Director of Personel, spoke to Saffron, too, "Sorry, but we hadn't considered Keahi because he's off in Boston."

"No he's not," Saffron found herself saying, "you can find him at the Silver Sands Hotel up in Pali. You should move quickly, though. I don't know how much longer he'll be in town."

The directors glanced at each other. Keahi had come back recently and performed a life-saving operation on a local child. They knew he was a good fit, and a spark of hope had ignited in their eyes.

"I'll bet you'd like to have him back in town, too, eh, Saffron?" Makani asked, a knowing grin on his face.

"Doesn't matter to me, one way or the other," Saffron said coldly.

Makani blinked with surprise, but all he said was, "That's a great idea. We'll see if we can contact him."

Saffron walked over and took Makani's pen. On the pad of paper in front of him, she wrote Keahi's cell phone number.

"We need surgery services," she said as she left the room, "I hope you'll do everything you can to keep them here."

———

BACK ON THE SET, Saffron was grateful to step into Gwen Thistledown's shoes again. This time, she delivered sage advice to Elyse's character to "follow her heart." It was the impetus that led the lead character to break up with Adam—the other man.

Gwen had been souvenir shopping and was carting a large bag full of knickknacks, leis, and kukui nut keychains, and Saffron tugged at it absentmindedly while she stood at the edge of the set.

She watched Elias Blum carefully, both for her cues and for any signs that he was reacting to Shar's death in any way. Other than his pretzeling around the director's chair, Blum seemed fine. He seemed, in fact, exactly as he had every other day.

Saffron wondered if that was a sign of guilt. But naming Blum as a suspect had the same problem as naming the actors: Killing Shar got in the way of what they wanted most, which seemed to be finishing this movie. If Blum had wanted rid of her, he could simply have fired her.

No, even though Blum had been in a relationship with Shar, he just didn't fit as a good suspect. Whoever had killed Shar must have known something about her routine, must have known she'd use the lead, must have had a compelling reason to want the woman gone. And looking at Blum's lined, leathery face, Saffron doubted he knew his way around a makeup kit.

Saffron kept coming back to Roman. He checked all the boxes: he knew makeup, he knew Shar, and he had something to gain by her death. In fact, he was on set now, buzzing around, touching up Zayne's makeup, patting Elyse's hair into place.

Saffron tried to think how she could possibly get more information on him. Every time she approached him, he put up a wall. His answers were short and guarded. He avoided her if he could.

Ace was on set, today, too. He was in the scene as Zayne's kooky best friend. She wondered if Zayne knew that Ace was working with Rossi. She wanted to tell the star, but was half-afraid of what he'd do to Ace if she did.

Mano, Slate, and the Empress had finagled their way to the edge of the set again, and Saffron cast them a smile as she awaited her cue. Last night, after Holly had gone home and Saffron was alone, she'd listened to Rossi's recording of her breakup with Nik. It had made her cry again, and she'd gone to sleep with the realization that in the space of a week, she'd lost both of the men she'd cared most about. That seemed cause for some serious introspection.

She couldn't deny that she'd had a hand in losing both of them. She'd encouraged Keahi to go back to Boston and become a surgeon again. She'd known at the time that it was right, but now she wondered if she should have insisted he stay and keep working at the luau. And when he'd invited her, last Christmas Eve, to return with him to the mainland, maybe she should have given it more thought.

She'd never held Nik back, either. When he wanted to go to Barbados on a surfing trip, she'd supported him. And when he decided to go on the semi-professional circuit, she'd encouraged him.

Even her first boyfriend, back in Washington, DC, Reggie, who had worked for a medical supply company, had failed to convince her to come with him when he was transferred to the Honolulu office.

She hadn't thought of Reggie in a long time. He'd told her he needed a little more chaos in his life, and at the time, she couldn't have imagined allowing any into hers. She wondered, briefly, if he was still in Honolulu. He would be surprised to know she had moved to Hawaii after all, and that she had embraced chaos since they'd last spoken.

Last night she realized that she seemed forever doomed to help the men she loved find happiness elsewhere, and she'd fallen asleep feeling absolutely alone.

Today, though, in the bright street of what was now her hometown, with three staunch supporters waving at her from the sidelines, she realized that nothing could be further from the truth. She may not have Reggie, or Keahi, or Nik, but she wasn't alone. She had her 'ohana—her family. While it didn't erase the pain, it did ease it.

"Gwen! Gwen!" Saffron dimly registered that someone was shouting in her direction, and she looked over at Elias Blum for a long moment before she remembered that was what he thought her name was.

"Yes, sorry, Mr. Blum?"

"I want to know what you think of this line. You have good instincts."

"Sure," Saffron crossed to him and watched as he started the scene between Adam and Elyse again. Her jaw tightened as she heard Elyse deliver the line in question.

"We're not working," she said, and Adam's face showed a perfectly accurate mix of disbelief and disappointment. To Saffron, it was like looking in a mirror.

"CUT!" Blum bellowed, then looked at Saffron expectantly. In fact, everyone looked at Saffron expectantly.

"Well, Gwen, what do you think?" Blum demanded. "Does that sound, I don't know, believable? Authentic? Would someone say that to end a relationship?"

Saffron looked around. This fabricated world, these pretend people. What did any of them know about authenticity? Her gaze landed on Ace Carnation, whose narrowed eyes and slumped shoulders told her that he knew that she knew where he had gotten the line he'd added to the script to impress Blum.

She answered Blum, but kept her gaze locked on Ace as she replied, "It sounds completely authentic to me."

"Alright then, let's roll it again," Blum dismissed her with a wave of his hand, and Ace shrugged an apology in her direction.

Nobody else knew, at least nobody here, that Ace had snatched a little part of her life and splashed it onto the big screen. Elyse seemed unconcerned, Adam oblivious. Kirk, Elyse's accountant, sat reading a book off to the side of the set, and he didn't seem at all interested in anything that was happening.

Though Saffron couldn't see the title of the book, she did recognize the sticker on its spine. It was a bright red starburst denoting that he had bought it at Heluhelu Here, the local bookshop. Saffron made a mental note to visit it and see what books the accountant had picked up.

Chapter Twelve

L ate in the afternoon, Saffron stood for the fifth take of her "Follow your heart," line. Blum had passed the point of annoyance and was teetering on the edge of full fury.

"No, no, no! Say it like you mean it, Gwen!"

"Sorry, Mr. Blum," Saffron mumbled. She had tried, had

really tried, to put her soul into the last take, but even she recognized that the line was coming out flat.

"Don't be sorry, be sensational! Why are you not convincing Elyse that she should follow her heart?"

"I don't know. Maybe—" Saffron stopped herself before she said any more.

"Maybe what?" Blum demanded.

Saffron was all out of restraint. She let the words fly, "Maybe she *shouldn't* follow her heart."

"Gwen!" Blum was shocked.

"No, really. Maybe I'm giving her terrible advice. Maybe she should marry Adam while she's got the chance, not run off after Zayne, who may not be the one for her anyway."

"Of course he is!" Blum bellowed.

"How do you know?" Saffron snapped back. She had left her spot, striding to the front edge of the boardwalk where Blum sat.

"Because it's in the script!" Blum's face was purple.

Saffron absorbed that. In the long moment of silence that followed, she heard a sharp cheeping. She looked down to see, pecking at the freckles on her feet, the little ebony puff that was Duchess. She looked up at the edge of the set, where the Empress raised her hands in apology.

Saffron reached down and scooped up the little chick, then dared to look back at Blum. She wasn't sure if he was staring at her incredulously or at the chick.

In silence, Blum untangled himself from his chair and stood. The crew all took an involuntary step back.

To Saffron's surprise, Blum gestured her over to him, then began to walk. She jogged along beside him, trying to keep up with his long strides.

"Gwen," he said, walking off down the boardwalk where nobody else hovered, "I sense you're upset."

Saffron didn't respond. It seemed unprofessional at the

least to air her current heartaches. She simply stroked the little chick in silence. It was downy soft and settled happily into her hands. Luckily, Blum was already making assumptions.

"I understand that it was you who found our makeup artist dead. I'm truly sorry about that."

"Sorry I found her, or sorry that she's dead?" Saffron's tone was harsher than she intended.

"Both," he said simply. "Not many people know, but I was quite fond of Shar. She lived life loud, if you know what I mean."

Saffron thought of the leopard-print high heels and did know what he meant.

"And I think I'm mourning her, in my way," he said thoughtfully, "and probably will be for a long time to come."

"But you have to shove that aside right now so you can finish the movie?" Saffron finished for him.

Blum stopped right in the middle of the boardwalk. He turned an astonished face to Saffron.

"Oh, no, no, no."

"No?"

"No. These last few days I've been truly exploring the depth of my grief. I've been thinking about what I could have done, what I should have done, what might have made my time with her more meaningful."

"You have?" it was hard to imagine all that going on behind his stoic exterior.

"I have. And I've been infusing that grief, that guilt, and the joy of my few short months with her into the film. I've changed lighting, I've changed dialogue, I've tried to add into the script a little of the dark and the bitter so that the happy ending will be even more bright and sweet. That's what you bring to this scene, Gwen, that little glimmer of hope that even though Elyse's character has to go through this dark moment, there may be sunshine ahead for her." He turned and put both hands on Saffron's shoulders, "You guide the audience to the happy ending, Gwen. They can't get there without you."

Duchess had fallen asleep in her hands and was rattling off a chirpy little snore. Suddenly, and explosively, Blum laughed.

"Leave your little friend with me, and we'll try the scene again," he said, scooping Duchess into the protective bowl of his long fingers.

They went back to the set, and he climbed back into his chair. Duchess awoke, settled onto his knee, and watched the proceedings attentively.

The last take of the day was smooth. Easy. Perfect. Saffron didn't try to ignore the pain Elyse's character was going to go through when breaking up with Adam, she embraced it. She embraced it and chose to believe in happiness ahead anyway. When she told the green-eyed actress to follow her heart, Saffron was really speaking to herself.

———

THE BOOKSHOP WAS dim and quiet when Saffron made her way inside that evening. A book club was going on in the back room, and some laughter trickled out, but the shelves muffled it, and the proprietors of the shop didn't seem to notice it at all.

Viola and Arnold Arrowood spent their days on the over-stuffed couch behind the counter, reading. They barely spoke to each other, and despised speaking to customers. Regulars at the bookshop knew to write down their name and their purchases on the pad of paper at the register, make their own change, and leave quietly.

Saffron had no intention of allowing them their uninter-rupted reading time this evening.

"Hello, Viola," she said, jarring the very small woman out of a very large book on dutch-oven cookery.

Viola's eyes looked huge behind her enormous glasses.

"I need to know about a customer you've had here in the last couple of days," Saffron said, "a man with glasses, a little bit of a beard, wispy hair, probably carrying a briefcase."

Viola shrugged her slight shoulders, "Do you know his name?" her voice was rusty, and Saffron realized that she probably hadn't used it for some time. She and Arnold communicated mostly through nods, nudges, and thick fingers underlining passages in their respective books.

"Yes. Kirk Marshall."

Viola poked a finger toward the counter, "Check the pad." The small woman immersed herself back into the world of dutch ovens.

Saffron flipped through the pages of the pad. There were several names she knew, and it was interesting to see what they'd bought. Belle Tucker, mother of the seven wild Tucker kids, had been into the shop and picked up a book entitled, "Serenity Now: Finding Calm in Chaos." Yesterday, Saffron's father, Slate, had purchased a copy of "Beach Yoga for Seniors," and Holly had taken home a whole set of "Sweet and Steamy Bakeshop Romance" novels.

When Kirk Marshall's tidy handwriting caught her eye, Saffron was disappointed. His reading list included a general history text and a dry-sounding tome about the sixteen personality types.

"His reading is as dull as he is," Saffron said.

"What did you expect him to read?" Viola didn't bother coming out from behind her book this time.

Saffron took a moment to picture what she'd been hoping to find, "I don't know, *Thirty-one Do-It-Yourself Poisons*," she said absently, sure that Viola wasn't really listening, "or *A Step-by-Step Guide to Getting Away with Murder*."

"Non-fiction," Viola said, her small finger pointing off to

the left of the dim room, amidst the towering shelves, "over there."

Saffron was tempted to go see if such books actually existed, but she had more to do tonight, "Thank you," she said, heading for the door.

"Wait!" Viola said, "You're in the movies now, huh?"

Saffron shrugged, "I guess I am."

"You'd better take that box by the front door. Get yourself some ideas for glamorous hairstyles and fabulous clothes. For your premier." Viola waved her hand at a musty box sitting atop a very old armchair by the door.

Saffron peeked inside. It appeared to be full of old celebrity gossip magazines. She had no interest in them, but it was rare for either of the Arrowoods to notice in anything that was not printed on a page, so Saffron hefted the box and thanked them again.

At home later, Saffron let Jasper out again. He was pretty great at keeping the place free of gawkers and photographers.

She glanced at the cottages. Their windows were dark, and no rental cars were outside. This would be the perfect time to collect towels and change sheets.

Saffron would have liked to go inside and eat the garlic shrimp and rice she'd picked up on her way home, but she'd put this off long enough, and the rent she made from the cottages really was a significant part of her income. She wanted to keep her excellent reputation for hostessing.

Ace's cottage was, as she had predicted, a mess. Just tidying and hauling out the trash took her half an hour. By the time she'd scrubbed the bathroom, changed the towels and sheets, and set the box of chocolate-dipped macadamia nuts on the table, the sun had set. Only an orange glow accompanied her to Zayne's cottage.

His was the opposite. It was nearly as tidy as the day he rented it. The bed didn't even look slept in. Saffron tidied it anyway and left the box of chocolates with a thank-you in her heart for tidy Zayne Grayson.

Saffron stopped short when she walked into Elyse's cottage. On the table in the middle of the front room was the enormous bouquet of flowers that had been delivered to her house.

Was this who Zayne had bought the flowers for? If so, it made sense why he couldn't have them delivered directly to her. The press would go wild for rumors of Zayne Grayson and Elyse Avery, onscreen flames, dating in real life.

But were they dating? He hadn't said so, exactly, and they certainly didn't seem particularly cozy on set. Maybe the flowers had simply been a token of his admiration for his co-star.

The night was fully dark outside now, and the crickets were playing their beautiful night songs. Saffron opened a window and let the night breeze play across the big bouquet, filling the cottage with the sweet scent of the flowers.

Elyse's cottage showed that she'd definitely been living there, but it wasn't overly messy. The only part that Saffron had to give more than a little attention to was the bathroom counter. Elyse had an extensive makeup kit of her own, and an entire closet full of clothes. Saffron realized again how much effort it must take to always look so polished and perfect.

Running the vacuum over the bedroom floor, Saffron bumped into the nightstand and heard a dull thud. She switched off the vacuum and went fishing under the bed for something she'd knocked off the stand.

It was a ring box—black velvet, as big as a bread roll. She knew she shouldn't open it, but her curiosity got the better of her and she snapped it open to reveal an exquisite diamond wedding set. The engagement ring was enormous, and the band below it encrusted with diamonds.

Saffron gasped. Where had this come from? She hadn't

seen anything in the magazines about Elyse having any particularly serious relationship. Could it be from Zayne? Or Adam?

Either way, she was sure she wasn't meant to be gawking at it. She looked instinctively at the window, afraid she'd see a camera there, but all was quiet tonight. She snapped the box closed and replaced it on the nightstand.

Maybe she had missed something. She went inside and lugged the big cardboard box into the living room. As she flipped through the magazines, she began to understand their draw.

It was like looking into someone else's life. As she ate her garlic shrimp, she explored the last several decades of movie history. Some of the magazines were recent, and some stretched back in time.

The fashions had changed. The stars looked much younger. But the stories were eerily similar, as if the magazines simply plugged in new names every few years.

But not even all the names were new. Saffron paused over a story with a familiar name: Elyse Avery, four years old at the time, cast in her first major role.

Saffron was intrigued to read that Elyse's beginnings had been humble and difficult. Saffron would never have guessed that the glamorous star had started out her life split up from her three siblings in the foster care system before landing with the wealthy, childless Averys of Hollywood. From then on, it seemed her life was charmed. It just went to show that happy endings did occur, even in the real world.

Saffron's phone rang and she jumped, tossing a shrimp and a magazine halfway across the room.

The Empress' resonant voice set Saffron at ease immediately.

"My dear, you must come to tea tomorrow afternoon. Say, four o'clock?"

Saffron pictured the quiet privacy of the Empress' mansion, "Of course. I'd love to."

"Excellent. Now, how are you doing? You had a grueling day on set."

"It was a little rough," Saffron admitted, "but it ended well."

"It did indeed. My Duchess seemed to know that you needed her comfort."

"Maybe she'll be as good as Princess at bringing a sense of calm," Saffron said. Nothing pleased the Empress more than hearing Princess praised.

"Oh, I do hope so. Now, tell me how you are faring this evening."

"I'm fine," she said, "everything's okay."

"I gathered today from my time with Mano that he still does not know his grandson is on the island?"

"I certainly haven't told him."

"Wise. Wise. You did a beautiful job with your line today."

"Thanks," Saffron shrugged off the compliment, "it's a little intimidating being there with all the real stars."

"Oh, hush now! You are a star if I've ever seen one!"

"Maybe you haven't seen enough stars," Saffron teased.

"I'll have you know that I spent this evening with a star— one you are very familiar with. And that's what I am calling to talk to you about."

Saffron waited. She heard the Empress take a deep breath, then plunge ahead.

"My dear, I know that you are having a difficult time in your love life just now, but I do not want you to see this Zayne Grayson anymore. He will only break your heart."

Saffron smiled at her concern. She must not have heard the whole story behind the misleading pictures, "Oh, don't worry, there's nothing going on. That was just a big lie cooked up by the paparazzi."

"Thank heaven!" the Empress exploded, "because he's *married*!"

Saffron gasped, nearly inhaling a shrimp, "He's what? How do you know?"

"Because I am selling him a house I own out on one of the points south of here, it was my husband, Nelson's, grandfather's house, you know, and on the paperwork I received, Zayne Grayson had marked 'Married!'"

Married? Could this be why Zayne was never seen with anyone on the red carpet? Saffron snatched some of the magazines and turned to the photos of Zayne. None of them showed him wearing a wedding ring, but in one, on the ring finger of his left hand, she thought she saw a thin band of slightly less-tanned skin, as if he had been wearing a ring at one point, but then he had taken it off before the cameras could catch it.

And then she knew.

The rings in Elyse's bungalow. The unused bed in Zayne's. Zayne and Elyse were carrying on a secret marriage.

Chapter Thirteen

Saffron wasn't sure what to do with the new information about Zayne and Elyse. Upon further reflection, she realized that it really was none of her business, and that the best thing she could do was pretend she knew nothing about it.

The next morning, though, as the storm clouds were gathering over the mountain behind the farm and she was returning from the egg house, leading Jasper with a donkey cart full of eggs and his best friend, Claudette the hen, on his back, that strategy became completely impossible.

The cottages each had their lights on, and Zayne tossed Saffron a wave from his front window as she passed his cottage. He came out on the lanai to call a thanks to her for leaving the chocolates. He held up the box and Saffron shouted, "You're welcome!"

At the same moment, Elyse's front door opened and Kirk Marshall stepped out, his briefcase in hand, straightening his tie.

Saffron heard a sound from Zayne, like he'd been punched. Kirk turned and saw him, then fled down the steps as fast as he could go, heading for a little gold car that Saffron hadn't seen before.

"Hey!" Zayne cried, vaulting over the railing of his lanai, "Hey! What did I tell you? Stay away from her! If she needs financial advice, she'll call you on the phone!"

Kirk scrambled for the car door, terror on his face, and Zayne bolted across the lawn, sending the box of chocolates sailing toward the small man's head.

"I've had enough of you!" Zayne shouted, "You little creep! Stay away from her, or I'll break every bone in your scrawny body!"

Saffron was glad the paparazzi hadn't shown up yet this morning. This would be front-page stuff. At least she hoped they hadn't. She scanned the bushes, but didn't see any gleaming round lenses.

Elyse was out in the yard now, shouting at Zayne, "Stop it! Leave him alone!"

Zayne whirled on her, "Leave him alone? Why don't you leave him alone?"

"Zayne!" she countered, "I've told you—it's complicated."

He threw his arms up, "At least admit to me that he's not your accountant!"

"What are you talking about?" Elyse turned back toward the cottage. Even from here Saffron could see that she was trembling.

"I'm talking about the fact that nobody needs to discuss their stock portfolio all night long. Nobody needs a financial consultation in their private trailer on set. If you want him, go ahead, but I'm not going to play your fool anymore."

"What I do is none of your business," Elyse said, jerking her head in Saffron's direction. Saffron was stuck. She'd like to slip into the house and let them have their fight in private, but they were between her and the house, and turning Jasper and the cart around to go back to the barn would draw far too much attention to herself. So she just stood there, trying to pretend she was gazing at the plumeria tree.

"If that's what you really think," Zayne said, "then that's fine with me. It's not like I'm getting a whole lot out of this. But he's using you, Elyse, and I can't figure out why you're letting him."

Elyse stomped up the steps of her lanai and slammed the door behind her.

Zayne looked at Saffron, threw his arms up in defeat, and stalked back to his cottage.

Saffron looked at Jasper, whose big ears were all a-swivel from the shouting. He stomped a hoof and snorted. Claudette bawked a reprimand toward the departing actor.

Just then, the skies opened and rain began to fall hard and fast. Saffron raced to the steps, pulling the cartons from the donkey cart and jamming them in the avocado-colored fridge. It took several trips across the lanai to empty the cart.

Then she jumped in it and clucked to Jasper. He was already soaked, his curly gray hair streaming, and he took off for the barn so fast that Saffron had to hold on to the armrests on the cart.

Saffron, Jasper, and Claudette all breathed a sigh of relief as they careened into the open doors of the barn and were greeted by the fresh smell of dry hay and dust.

Little rivulets of water ran down Saffron's temples and back, dripping off her fingertips as she unharnessed Jasper and put him in his stall. There, she grabbed a towel and started to dry him off. She gave Claudette a couple of swipes, too.

A small sound caught her attention. She didn't turn, but she spoke loudly when she said, "You just can't help yourself, can you?"

There was no answer.

"Rossi, I know you're there. What I don't know is why in

the world you would want a picture of me drying off my donkey."

"It's all part of the story," came the voice. He was in the loft, or rather his legs were in the loft and the rest of him was hanging down from it, camera in front of his face.

"Don't sue me if you fall out of there," she said coldly, giving Jasper one last pat.

Rossi swung up and climbed down the ladder, "No promises," he said. She could tell he was attempting a joke, but she wasn't in a laughing mood.

The rain hammered the tin roof above them, and Saffron realized they weren't going anywhere for a while. She took the damp towel and started to wipe down the cart.

"So, why do you do this?" she asked, "Why do you invade people's privacy, tell lies about them, haunt their every move?"

He chuckled, "Oh, I never tire of the American public's sweet naïveté."

Saffron whirled on him, "*It's just how it is*, you're going to say, *It's not your fault?*"

"No, I'm going to say that paparazzi aren't the bad guys. It's not like we're working alone here. Many celebrities call *us* when they're going to be somewhere—they send us a text to come capture them. We're essential to keeping them relevant, seen, desired."

"That may be true for some, but what is your obsession with Zayne Grayson? You can't pretend that you're doing him some big favor—he obviously doesn't want you taking photos of him."

Rossi sat down on a bale of hay, letting his camera drop to his chest. He looked older up close, more worn. It was the first time Saffron thought that maybe his job wasn't easy for him, either. "Listen, I know better than anyone that I am obsessed with Zayne Grayson. But that is because he's hiding something from me, and I'm going to find out what that is at any cost."

Saffron breathed a soft sigh of relief—he obviously hadn't seen what had just happened out on the other side of the house. Maybe Zayne's secret was safe for one more day.

"Any cost?"

"*Any* cost."

"Even though he doesn't want you to? Even though there might be things he doesn't want the world to know? Doesn't he have that right? To keep some things secret?"

"Not from me."

"Why not from you?"

"Because I made Zayne Grayson. Back when I was a legitimate studio photographer, when I got invites to all the posh parties and a place on the velvet rope at all the red-carpet walks. I took the photo that made the world love Zayne Grayson, when he was thirteen and awkward. I caught him in a casual moment with his mother, and from then on his rise to stardom was meteoric."

"What happened?"

"His parents were divorced. His father didn't like that the mother was in the photo that was making Zayne famous. He called the studio, pulled some strings, pretty soon I couldn't get anyone over there to answer my calls. Been chasing celebs through alleyways and standing in the rain outside nightclubs ever since."

"So you think Zayne owes you some kind of, redemption for what his father did?"

"Listen, one of these days, I'm going to figure out what he's hiding, and when I do, and when I break that story wide open, I'm going to get six figures for those photos. And then I'm going to retire. Somewhere comfortable. No more sleeping in barn lofts. No more shivering in the back of my car. And then Zayne can do whatever he wants."

"No, I get it," Saffron held up her hands and sat down on

the cart, facing Rossi, "Zayne owes you. So what's your excuse for invading *my* privacy?"

"I don't know what you're talking about," Rossi hedged.

"I have your recorder. I know you were listening in on my conversation with my boyfriend."

"Ex-boyfriend?" Rossi's smile was cruel.

Saffron didn't blink, "Ex-boyfriend."

"Look, don't take it personal. I'm no different from Elias Blum."

"Excuse me?"

"We both tell stories. Sometimes, they're a little more fiction than truth, but our audiences eat them up."

"There's no comparison," Saffron spat. Jasper let out an angry honk.

"Don't let that thing out," Rossi said, "It hates me."

"I don't think he's the only one. Now, I suggest you rent a room in town, or, even better, get on a plane and go home. You're not staying in my barn another minute." Saffron stood and pointed to the door. For a couple of heartbeats, she was afraid he would resist, maybe even get violent, but instead, he sighed.

"Just let me get my stuff from the loft," he said, resigned. He climbed up, rustled around, and climbed back down wearing a raincoat and carrying a backpack. He'd stowed his camera inside, and he trudged out into the heavy rain. Saffron had no doubt that she would see him again.

LATER THAT MORNING, when the rain had lessened, Saffron sat in her kitchen listening to the steady patter on the ground outside.

Filming had been called off for the day, but Blum wanted everyone working still. For the principal actors, there would be costume fittings and makeup trials and dialogue coaching throughout the day. Blum sent the crew out to them at the egg farm, and there had been a steady stream of visitors all day. Cast and crew played cards on the screened back lanai of Ace's cottage. Adam visited Elyse, then later, a cadre of costume designers hauled garment bags into her cottage, ostensibly for her to try on. Roman showed up with his bag full of grocery store makeup to try out some different looks. Saffron wondered if he'd be relieved to see Elyse's extensive kit. Maybe she'd let him use it since he didn't have access to his own. Amidst all the bustle in the yard, Saffron was relieved to be able to sit in her bungalow and relax with a cup of pineapple tea.

She leafed through the magazines, finding more photos of Zayne and Elyse through the years, and even a few of Ace.

His career had certainly taken a strange turn. He'd started out with some decent roles, but after he played the comic relief in one particularly popular movie two decades ago, he'd never gotten any other types of roles.

She read about Elias Blum and his movies as well as his social activism.

She perused the pictures and read the articles and wondered the whole time if Rossi had been right. Though she hated to admit it, there was some value to the actors in the magazines—these photos humanized them, gave them an image, a brand.

As the afternoon wore on, the clouds rolled back in and the traffic from the set slowed, then dried up all together. The rain began to pour again.

Later, she would shudder to think what may have happened if she hadn't gone to the sink to rinse her cup at just the moment she did. If she hadn't paused and looked up through the window above the sink, if she hadn't seen the little scrap of fluttering fabric.

But she did see it, and she went out onto the lanai to investigate. It was then that she saw, tumbled over the railing of her lanai, mostly hidden by the star jasmine plant that grew there, Elyse Avery.

Saffron ran to her, kneeling in the mud beside the still form.

"No, no, no," she was chanting, "Elyse? Elyse? You've got to open your eyes! Wake up, Elyse. Wake up!"

In the pouring rain, Elyse's face was shining silver. Saffron's color vision told her that there was something deeply wrong—under the silver was a watery blue. Elyse's lips and eyelids shimmered with that misty periwinkle undertone. Saffron had seen it before—only deeper and more permanent. This was life and death.

She felt for a pulse, and it was there, but it was weak and irregular. Saffron stood and ran for Zayne's cottage. She pounded on the front door, then whipped out her keys and let herself in, screaming his name.

But Zayne was nowhere to be found. The cottage was empty. She ran for Ace's cottage and he answered in a tee shirt and his stocking feet. When she gasped out what was wrong, he didn't hesitate, just charged out in the wet yard as he was, without stopping to find his shoes.

Saffron ran and pulled her car around, and Ace lifted Elyse from the bushes and set her in the front seat. Saffron drove like mad for the hospital, the rain turning her windshield into an undulating panel of molten silver.

She could barely see, could barely keep the car on the road atop the pooling remnants of the torrential downpour, and when she arrived at the entrance to the emergency room, she herself was shaking violently from the drenching she'd gotten while she was trying to find help.

A triage team came and whisked Elyse away on a stretcher. Saffron screamed at them, "She needs oxygen! She's suffocating!"

Makani Kawai, catching sight of Saffron standing outside the Emergency Room doors in the pouring rain, came and led her inside, where he wrapped a warm blanket around her and coaxed her into sitting down with a cup of cocoa in the waiting room.

Chapter Fourteen

Shuffling papers, shuffling feet, the occasional scraping chair. Saffron sat listening to the sounds of the hospital waiting room.

She wasn't comfortable—nobody there was comfortable. All of them, from the old woman who'd brought her grown son in with stomach pains, to the young couple cradling a fussy toddler, would much rather be just about anywhere else.

Still, Saffron was glad someone was here for Elyse. Even if she didn't wake up, even if the star didn't know that Saffron was here, Saffron was still glad that Elyse wasn't all alone.

She had called Mano and Slate and asked them to go looking for Zayne, but they hadn't had any luck so far. Saffron didn't know who else to alert. Maybe the accountant, and maybe Elias Blum, but she didn't have contact information for either one of them.

When a woman in dark blue scrubs stepped out of the back and said her name, Saffron left the sodden blanket and the empty cocoa cup and followed her through a door into a long, white hallway.

"It's a good thing you brought her in when you did," the

nurse said, "even a few more minutes and we wouldn't have been able to save her."

The words chilled Saffron's blood.

"But you were? Right? Able to save her?"

The woman nodded, "Oh, yes, she's going to be just fine, and so is her baby."

"Baby?" Saffron squeaked. Glancing around, she half-expected to see Rossi pop out from behind a laundry cart and snap a photo. The paparazzi would go wild for this little tidbit of information.

"Yes, strong heartbeat, strong responses, there's really nothing at all to worry about, other than the slight shock Ms. Avery underwent when we informed her that she was pregnant."

"Elyse didn't know, either?"

The nurse shook her head. "No, it was certainly a surprise to her."

Saffron glanced into the rooms they were passing, wondering what she would say to Elyse when she saw her. The woman hadn't been particularly warm toward her since Rossi's pictures had been published. If, as Saffron suspected, Elyse and Zayne were secretly married, Saffron couldn't blame her.

It turned out, however, that Saffron needn't have worried what she was going to say to Elyse. The nurse wasn't leading her to Elyse's room at all. The woman stopped in the center of the hall and held out an arm, indicating a small room to the left, "Miss Skye, our medical examiner and local law enforcement would like to ask you some questions."

Saffron stared into the room, where Arlene Winn, the slick-haired medical examiner, sat with a grumpy-looking Bradley on one side of a stark white table.

"I'm sorry, what?"

The medical examiner stood and stepped into the hall,

"Miss Skye, if you would please come willingly, I won't be forced to have Officer Bradley here arrest you."

Saffron felt weak as she walked in and sat down. She glanced at the clock on the wall. It was 2:30 AM.

Saffron had long ago learned that when you were in a room with faces as serious as these, you didn't start asking questions. She waited for Arlene to speak.

"Would you like to begin?" Arlene surprised her.

"I—I don't know what you'd like me to say."

"Maybe you could begin with an explanation of why you are, once again, the first person on the scene of a poisoning?"

"Poisoning?"

"Do you dabble in toxic substances, Miss Skye?"

"What? No, I—"

"Do you find the effect of chemicals and inhalants on the body a very interesting study?"

"Of course not!"

"Then tell me why you have, TWICE, been involved in cases of toxic substances."

"I don't know why," Saffron managed. "I didn't even know they were exposed to toxic substances until later. Is that what happened to Elyse, then?"

"Carbon Monoxide poisoning," Bradley said.

"What? I just had the cottages inspected last month," Saffron was trying to make sense of that. She'd been assured everything was safe and healthy for her guests. "And there's a detector."

"Oh, yeah, everything was set up just fine, but the CO2 detector and the hot water heater had been tampered with," Bradley said. "I was just out there. It's fixed now. Shouldn't be any more trouble."

"The question is," Arlene cut in, "who tampered with it in the first place?"

"What we need to know," Bradley rephrased, "Is who all might have had access to the cottage?"

Saffron thought through the fog of the last 24 hours, "I'm not sure," she said hesitantly.

"Listen, Miss Skye, for whatever reason, Officer Bradley here is reluctant to take you into custody. But unless you can offer me some reason to think that someone else may be responsible for this, I'm going to have to go over his head and call in the Honolulu officers to take over."

Bradley shifted. He didn't like that idea any more than Saffron did.

"The reason I don't know is that there were tons of people in and out of the cottage yesterday," Saffron rubbed her temples, "Elyse, of course, and her accountant, and Adam Sullivan, and maybe Zayne Grayson, and Roman the makeup guy, and about six costumers, and maybe a dialogue coach or two, and a couple of production assistants, and maybe more people. I honestly wasn't watching the cottage every minute."

"Do you have any evidence that any one of those people might have been angry with the victim?" Arlene pressed.

"Sure," Saffron said, her head feeling slightly swimmy, "I mean, any of them—Adam has been wanting her attention, but she's been rejecting him, Zayne's upset she's been seeing her accountant, Roman and the costumers seemed annoyed they had to come all the way out to the farm in the rain, and then there's the fact that plenty of people just dislike her because she's beautiful and successful."

"Are you one of those people?" Arlene leaned forward.

"Of course not!"

"You do admit that it's strange that I've had two poisoning victims in this hospital in the last few days, and you have been the first person to find both of them?" Arlene demanded.

"I don't like it any more than you do," Saffron said.

"How did you know she was hypoxic?" Arlene's tone was accusing.

"I'm sorry?" Saffron wasn't familiar with the term.

"You diagnosed Ms. Avery's condition accurately when you shouted at the triage nurses that she needed oxygen—she was hypoxic. How did you know that?"

"Her skin," Saffron said, "she had a bluish cast, like a mist, over her lips and eyelids."

Arlene tossed her arms in the air, annoyed, "There she goes again, claiming to see things nobody else can see. The level of oxygen deprivation that the patient had undergone when she arrived could not be seen by the naked eye."

Bradley cleared his throat, then waited a long moment, until Arlene Winn looked at him, "Saffron's ability to see color is one of the wonders of the world, Ms. Winn."

Clearly, Arlene Winn had expected more support from the officer.

"So you think she's telling the truth? That she's innocent?"

"I do."

"And you aren't the least concerned that we have two poisoning victims and no suspects?"

"We never said we had no suspects," Bradley said, "Just that Saffron isn't one of them."

Arlene Winn looked back and forth between them.

"The longer we sit here," Saffron said, "The more likely that the real killer gets away."

"Give me one good reason why I shouldn't suspect you," Arlene challenged.

Saffron narrowed her eyes, "Because if I had wanted to kill her, I wouldn't have driven her to the hospital on treacherous roads in the middle of the night."

She saw the gleam in Bradley's eye and the begrudging acceptance in Arlene's.

"Alright then, but if the paperwork isn't filed tomorrow, I'm calling Honolulu myself."

Saffron nodded, "Fair enough." Bradley seemed surprised she would acquiesce. She held up a hand, "But I have a few questions for you, too, Ms. Winn."

The woman looked both surprised and wary. She didn't agree, but she didn't refuse, either, so Saffron plunged on.

"I just want to be clear. Shar was poisoned, too?"

"I thought you knew all about that—the red lead, the makeup kit."

"And it makes sense that the powder became airborne, because to kill someone by just having them use the blush would take a long time."

"Yes, the powder would have to soak into the skin a little at a time. But indications in the victim's body suggest that she inhaled a large amount of the dust at once—which seems consistent with the speckles of it you found throughout the trailer. Very high lead levels can cause seizures, unconsciousness, and death. That seems to be what happened in this case."

"How come every answer we come up with leads us to two more questions," Bradley complained.

"What questions do you have now?" Arlene asked.

"How did it get airborne and who was responsible?" Saffron said.

Arlene sniffed, "Well at least we can agree on one thing—we need to find those answers."

INSIDE THE COTTAGE back at the egg farm, things looked very much like they had when Saffron had cleaned up.

Other than some used tumblers in the sink and some of Elyse's clothes on the floor in the bathroom, the place still looked tidy.

Saffron looked through the rooms, willing something to jump out at her. She wasn't sure what she expected, but some kind of calling card from Elyse's would-be killer.

Bradley had talked to her after the interrogation and detailed the ways in which the hot water heater had been tampered with. Though he assured her all had been put right and everything was safe now, Saffron kept the windows and the front and back doors open, just to feel the cold air pushing through.

The gas that had poisoned Elyse had been silent and unde-tectable. It had built up inside the cottage that evening after everyone had left, when Elyse had closed the door and windows, when she thought she was most safe. It had no scent, no sound, and, most terrifying to Saffron, no color. She wouldn't know if it was in the room with her until it was too late.

It was, in that way, like the killer.

She shivered involuntarily and redoubled her efforts. She wished there was a way to review the day, to simply stand here and rewind the comings and goings of Elyse's visitors as they came for costume fittings or makeup sessions.

Saffron wandered through the rooms of the cottage, looking for anything left behind.

She glanced at the nightstand, expecting to glimpse the ring box. It wasn't there. Saffron checked under the bed and in the drawer. Nothing. She tried to remember if Elyse had been wearing the ring, but couldn't picture it on her blue-tinged hand. She was relatively sure it hadn't been with the star.

Had Elyse put it away for safe-keeping, or had someone taken it? Another question Saffron didn't know how to answer.

Saffron checked the bathroom—the makeup kit still sat spread out on the counter. She searched it again, but found nothing out of the ordinary.

She slipped into the back of the cottage and opened the closet that held the furnace and water heater.

Saffron froze, her eyes fixed on a smudge just inside the doorjamb of the closet.

Had Bradley seen this? If so, he hadn't mentioned it. She pulled out her cell phone and snapped a photo of it: a minium-red smudge about as long as her index finger. There was no other red like it. Saffron was certain that it was the same powder that had killed Shar.

There were no other traces of it here, though. No speckles, no piles of it mixed with the copious dust on the floor of the closet. Saffron crouched down and reached a hand toward the pilot light of the water heater. To tamper with it, she'd have to kneel here and reach inside. Her knee brushed the doorjamb in just the same place as the smudge.

The minium, she reasoned, must have been on the killer's clothes. That was consistent with the idea that it had been in the air. They probably weren't even aware it was on them. But now that Saffron was, she would be keeping an eye out for that tell-tale red dust.

THE SET WAS DRENCHED when Saffron pulled up to it the next day, still looking for Zayne. The catering vans were all locked up, the cameras and mics all put away. She climbed out with her rainbow umbrella hoisted over her.

Hawaii was beautiful when the sun shone, but there was a special elegance about it when the rain fell. The colors of the island, usually so bright and vivid, mellowed when it rained. The boardwalk deepened from toffee colored to warm choco-late, the blueberry and lemon storefronts became rich sapphire and goldenrod. The sky, usually clear and saturated with blue, washed out to a misty pearl gray.

It was like a rest to Saffron's eyes. In the same way that a massage brought a sense of calm and relaxation to some people, the muted colors soothed Saffron. Even with the turmoil of the last few days, the rain brought a tranquility that gave Saffron strength.

Holoholo street was still blocked off and it felt like a ghost town. The usually bustling boardwalk was empty, the shops, though open, were completely deserted. Saffron's friend, Fumi, had confided that the shop owners had all been paid very well for the time it would take to shoot the film. They were considering it a paid vacation.

The only movement came from the feral chicken family that Saffron had seen the other day. They seemed completely unconcerned about the rain, and were enjoying pecking at the leaves of a bush along the boardwalk.

Saffron knocked at the door of Zayne's trailer. He hadn't been at the cottage, and this was the only other place she could think of to look for him. There was no answer. She tried the door handle, but it was locked. No lights were on inside, and she didn't see any shifting in the trailer as she stood watching it, so she was relatively sure nobody was inside.

Adam's trailer was the opposite. Light streamed out of the windows and the sound of the TV drifted through the rainy morning. Saffron knocked firmly.

When Adam opened the door, Saffron stepped back, "Hi Adam, have you seen Zayne?"

He blinked, as if slightly annoyed that she, along with everyone else, was overlooking him in favor of the other actor. She tried to explain further, "I mean, I need to give him a message."

"No, I haven't seen him since early yesterday," Adam said, "when I was out at your egg farm."

"Okay," she stood thinking about her next move.

"Saffron, come in out of the rain for a minute," he held the door wide.

Saffron wouldn't mind seeing the inside of another of these trailers. Once inside, Saffron was very aware of her dripping umbrella. His trailer was even more opulent than Elyse's had been, with hardwood floors and a miniature chandelier over the dining set. She set the dripping rainbow umbrella beside the door, an apology on her lips.

"Don't worry about it," Adam waved her off, "I've been tracking mud in and out all day."

And it was true. There were footprints made with the damp golden sand leading in and out of the front door, across the room to an enormous beanbag in the living area. Where Elyse had placed couches and a coffee table, Adam had devoted the room to the big beanbag.

He saw her staring at it, "Isn't it great?" he asked. Without warning, Adam ran over and did a flying leap onto it, landing with a squishy thump.

"I had it made in Honolulu especially for this shoot. Although," he admitted, "It hasn't been as well-used on this set as I'd like." He seemed disgruntled by that fact.

"How come?" Saffron asked.

"Well, you know, the people just haven't been as friendly on this set. Some sets, you've got crew and actors coming in and out all the time, people ready to party, hang out, go out. It hasn't been that way on this set."

"Why not?"

Adam shrugged, "Blum, I guess. He's pretty high-strung. Everybody knows we're here to work, not play. And," he began to say something else, but seemed to stop himself.

"No," Saffron urged, "What were you going to say?"

"Just that, I guess, there's probably a little more to it."

"What?"

"Oh, I don't know, the feeling on set is often really influenced by the principal actors. If they're cool, and chill, then everybody else is, too."

"But Elyse and Zayne aren't? Chill?"

Adam let out a low whistle, "Naw, I wouldn't say so."

"How come?"

"I don't know. They took off and stayed out at your farm all by themselves, as if they were just too good for the resort the studio put us up in. They barely speak to each other, spend all their free time in their own trailers. I sense there may be some history between them, or their relationship may be complicated somehow."

Saffron bit her lip to keep from saying, *You have no idea how complicated that relationship is.*

"So, it just makes it, weird, you know," Adam sighed, "Add to that all the paparazzi lurking in the shadows, and Ace Carnation constantly trying to wheedle his way into being friends with the director or the stars, it's just been a weird set, that's all."

Saffron nodded her understanding.

"But never mind that, come on over and try out the beanbag!"

There was nothing else to do. Unless she wanted to sit in the straight-backed dining chairs, which were pretty far away to have a decent conversation with Adam, there was no other place to sit.

Saffron perched on the edge of the beanbag, feeling the foam cubes inside compress beneath her. It was only a matter of time until it shifted under her and she slowly sank, rolling onto her back.

It was hard to remain ridged on the surface.

Adam chuckled, "Just relax, Saffron. It's a beanbag."

Saffron shifted onto her side. The beanbag was so vast that Adam was actually farther away than he would have been if they'd been on a couch, but laying there facing him introduced a much more intimate feel than sitting on regular furniture would have.

She tried to seem nonchalant, "So, I saw what you meant about not fighting the paparazzi."

A shadow crossed behind Adam's eyes, but he blinked it away, "If you're going to be in movies, it's something you've got to learn. I just wish I'd learned it a little sooner, and with a little less public coverage."

"I can see why it upsets you. Is it that way all the time?"

"Pretty much. I mean, if I'm not working on a movie, it eases up a little. As long as there's something in the works, they're looking for stories to tie it to."

Saffron considered that, "Do you ever take a break from filming just to have a break from them?"

"Sure. I've done it a couple times."

Saffron came out with her real question, "Adam, how far do you think the paparazzi would go to get a story? I mean, do you think they'd *hurt* someone?"

He regarded her in silence for several seconds longer than was comfortable. She wondered what he could be thinking.

"I think," he finally said, "that some of them would."

"Some of them? Like Rossi?"

Adam whistled again, "Yeah. Like him. That guy's crazy. Like being up on the roof in that rain yesterday."

"Roof?" Saffron asked in alarm.

"Yeah, on one of the cottages, the pink one."

Rossi had been on Elyse's roof yesterday?

"I thought everybody had seen him," Adam said, "We could hear him walking around, then we went out and saw him up there."

"What were you doing in Elyse's cottage?"

"Huh," he laughed a little, "you sound like Zayne."

"Just wondering."

"Running lines with the dialogue coach. I had to drive out

there, because Elyse is the queen and I'm just a member of the court."

Saffron remembered Roman's analogy about the hierarchy of Hollywood. She propped herself up with an elbow against the soft beanbag and mused, "If the stars are the monarchy, I wonder what the paparazzi are."

"Easy," Adam retorted, "they're the assassins."

Chapter Fifteen

W hen, after an hour in the beanbag, Adam invited
Saffron to get some lunch with him, she accepted.
He wanted some great local fare, and there was
only one place for that—the Oceanside Cafe.

He grabbed a jacket and they shared Saffron's rainbow
umbrella as they tripped down the boardwalk to the restaurant
at the edge of the beach.

The bell dinged as they pushed their way through the front door. The scent of onion rings enveloped them.

The Oceanside Cafe's onion rings were something special. They started with Maui onions, the sweetest onions on the planet, and ended with a salty/sweet dipping sauce that Bernadette, the Oceanside Cafe's owner, had invented. It was a blend of mango juice, brown sugar, soy sauce, and kiawe-wood-smoked sea salt. The result was a uniquely local sauce that Saffron craved.

Bernadette wasted no time seating them, and no time asking bluntly, "Where's Nik today?" The best thing about living in a small town was that everyone knew you and you always got plenty of support. The worst thing was that everyone knew you and you always got plenty of questions.

"Practicing for the big surfing competition," Saffron said confidently. Even if she hadn't seen him for a few days, she knew right where Nik would be.

Bernadette made a hmmm-cluck sound that reminded Saffron of a scolding her hens gave her when they were disappointed in her actions. She wanted to explain to Bernadette that Nik had broken up with her, not the other way around, but there was no way to do that with Adam here. She was just going to have to endure the woman's disapproval.

"Who's Nik?"

"He's—I mean, he *was*—my boyfriend."

"Aw. I'm sorry. Breakups stink."

A wave of emotion washed over Saffron. So much had been happening that she'd barely had time to really let the breakup sink in. But it had been days since she'd heard from Nik, and she suddenly missed his morning texts—shots of the sun breaking over his favorite surfing spots—and his goodnight phone calls. She missed the sense of adventure he always brought along with him. She missed the smell of the sea on his skin and the touch of his hand on hers.

She swallowed hard. Adam must have noticed.

"Fresh, huh?"

Saffron nodded.

"You know what helps a breakup more than anything?"

She shook her head, still fighting the lump in her throat.

"Thinking about your ex realistically. I mean, when you break up, you just remember all the good stuff, but not the stuff that didn't fit or didn't work or just drove you crazy about them. Anything about this Nik guy that didn't thrill you?"

Saffron thought about that momentarily. It seemed mean to talk about Nik's foibles, but there was some truth in what Adam was saying. She was idealizing their relationship somewhat.

"Well, I mean, he was a bit more of an adrenaline junkie than I am."

"Great! See?" Adam threw his hands up, spreading them wide over the table, "He may have been a great guy, but maybe not a great *match*."

Bernadette came back and thumped two glasses of water on the table. Saffron attempted a smile at her, but Bernadette was not so easily distracted, "What you want?" she demanded.

Saffron ordered one of the new items on the menu: ham and ginger sliders, with onion rings, of course. Adam, at Saffron's encouragement, tried the 'ono burger. Their food came quickly and they chatted about less weighty matters as they ate.

Saffron was dipping her last onion ring when she felt an eerie prickling on the back of her neck. She looked around with the increasingly familiar sensation that someone was watching her.

It took her several seconds to locate it, but finally she glimpsed, in the half-wall sized mirror across from their booth, the reflection of a round lens peering out from a hooded raincoat. Rossi was shooting photos of her and

Adam's reflection through the window on the far side of the restaurant.

Saffron stood and strode out. Somehow the switch from feeling sad over the breakup with Nik to feeling relieved by it had charged her with energy.

Rossi saw her coming. He ran.

Saffron ran, too. Out of the restaurant and down the boardwalk, then onto the beach. Rossi was running out of steam, she could see it.

"Hey!" she shouted, "Hey! Stop!"

He glanced back but kept running.

Saffron caught up with him when he hit the edge of the hala grove at the far North end of the beach.

The wet hala leaves were deep emerald green and the shadows within them a rich charcoal. The sand under their feet was umber rather than its usual glistening gold.

Rossi turned around like a cornered animal and, in a habitual defensive move, raised his camera.

Saffron thought of the images of Adam throwing his drink. They didn't represent the thoughtful person she'd spent the morning with. Adam was a good listener, a logical thinker.

The last thing she wanted was to give Rossi another story. Saffron stopped. She stared at him, crossing her arms.

Rossi seemed both disappointed and relieved.

"You're angry, no?" he called, breathing hard.

"You know the answer to that," Saffron was winded, too, and she sucked in the droplets of cool rain and sea spray gratefully.

"I have to work," he said, holding up one hand to the side of his camera, "I have to eat."

"You know," Saffron said, "I've seen your photographs. I have some old magazines, and I've noticed which ones were yours over the years. They're good. They have style and composition that other people's photos don't have."

Rossi peered out from behind the camera.

"Especially now, when a lot of the photos in the magazines are just sent in from bystanders with cell-phone cameras," Saffron said, "yours really stand out."

"I know," he replied.

"Then why don't you legitimize yourself?"

"What are you talking about?"

"Why don't you do portraiture? Scheduled shoots?"

"I told you, the studios don't call me anymore."

"Because you're a parasite."

"Hey!"

"It's true. Reframe what you do. Get stars' permission and stop trying to catch them at their worst. Instead, try to capture their best. You'll have people lined up all the way back to the mainland for your work."

The camera dipped down, and Saffron could see the man's whole face. There was a desperation there.

"And it's a lot easier to show people in a positive light than it is to show them in a negative one. You could work inside— no more climbing on slippery roofs."

He looked away, chagrined.

"And no more trying to trap people, or to hurt them," she watched for Rossi's reaction to that statement. To her surprise, he protested.

"I don't hurt people!"

"Sure you do. You harass them, make them afraid to live their lives, put them in danger."

"Anything they choose to do to avoid me is their own choice," Rossi stuck out his chin stubbornly.

That he could be so blind surprised Saffron. If he wouldn't admit that his actions were detrimental, could she ever get him to admit if he were the one who had hurt the two women? The scandalous stories of the two incidents would earn him recognition. It would be easy to sell photos of either event.

But there were two inconsistencies that made Saffron think Rossi might not be the sinister mastermind behind the poisonings: first, that she had not seen or heard of a tabloid story about Shar's death. Second, that Rossi was obsessed with Zayne. If he were going to orchestrate a horrible crime, Saffron would have guessed it would be directly connected to a story on Zayne. While Elyse was connected to Zayne, Rossi obviously didn't have any idea about that connection, because he hadn't broken the story of their secret marriage yet.

In fact, the only reason Rossi was shooting pictures of Saffron and Adam, she knew, was because of the story he'd concocted about her and Zayne. The headline for the photos he'd just taken would probably read, "ZAYNE'S NEW FLAME STEPPING OUT WITH CO-STAR!"

Rossi had lowered his camera.

"Leave me alone," Saffron said. "Leave us all alone." She turned to walk back up the beach and saw Adam standing at a distance, holding her rainbow umbrella, waiting for her. As she walked toward him, she heard, over the sound of the churning waves and falling rain, the click of Rossi's shutter.

IT WAS STILL RAINING that afternoon as Saffron sat in the Empress' lovely mansion and sipped coconut papaya tea.

"Your father informs me that you are no longer seeing Nik," the Empress' eyes held sympathy.

How many times would she have to confirm this? Saffron wasn't sure she was up to the task of not only enduring her breakup, but also informing everyone in Maika'i that she and Nik were not together anymore. That was part of the reason she'd told Slate and Mano—she'd been hoping they would spread the word so that she wouldn't have to.

"No, we broke up."

"Oh, my dear. What an incredibly difficult week."

Saffron nodded.

"And have you seen Keahi again?"

"Nope. No sign of him. From what I can tell, Mano still doesn't know he's on the island." Saffron didn't mention that she'd recommended the hospital administration reach out to Keahi. The more she thought about it, the more that had seemed like a foolish suggestion—Keahi wasn't likely to leave his prestigious job in Boston to come back here, and if by some miracle he did decide to, Saffron wasn't sure she could stand running into him and his new wife all over town.

She changed the subject and filled the Empress in on her terrible night at the hospital.

A breathless silence settled over the drawing room.

Princess tucked Duchess safely back under her fluffy white feathers, and the pair reminded Saffron of herself and the Empress. The Empress was a natural nurturer, a gentle woman with the soul of a warrior. She would, Saffron was convinced, go to any lengths to protect the ones she loved. Saffron was afraid she had said too much, had given the Empress too much to worry about.

"Will they still continue filming?" the Empress asked, "With Ms. Avery's traumatic experience?"

"Yes, she'll be out of the hospital tomorrow, which is our last day of rain. She didn't want anyone to know what had happened so as far as I know, the plan is to resume filming the next day as scheduled."

"My dear," the Empress said carefully, "perhaps you'd better bow out of your role in the film."

Saffron had expected the suggestion, but she still recoiled from it, "I couldn't. I-I want to finish. It wouldn't be fair to Blum to quit now, and it wouldn't be fair to Gwen."

"Gwen?" the Empress' carefully shaped eyebrows elevated, "the character?"

"She deserves her final scene," Saffron said, "I want to finish filming."

"It's too dangerous!" the Empress protested.

Saffron considered that, but she she had no good response for the Empress' assertion. "It may not matter anyway, if Zayne doesn't turn up."

"Mr. Grayson is missing?" the Empress gasped, and Princess echoed her with a wheezy cluck. Duchess gave a baby squeak that seemed to be the beginnings of the same sound.

"He seems to be. He's not at the cottage, nobody has seen him, and I have no idea how to reach him."

"Oh," the Empress exclaimed, then, turning to one of the two middle-aged men she employed as personal assistants, she cried, "Carlo! Carlo!"

Carlo entered quickly and inclined his head to ask what she needed.

"Bring me the papers on the desk in the upstairs study," she said, "the real estate papers."

When he returned with them, the Empress shuffled through the sheaf, then triumphantly offered one of the pages to Saffron.

"It's the purchase papers for the house I'm selling Mr. Grayson! His cell phone number is listed there!"

Saffron took the paper. The thought of just how much money one could get for these ten digits crossed her mind, but she pushed it aside. She was no Rossi.

She still didn't know if Zayne had even been informed that Elyse was in the hospital. She felt some obligation to tell him.

Springing up, she hugged the Empress.

"You're not involved with him, though?" the Empress's tone was warning.

"No! No! I told you—that was all fabricated."

"Alright then, go and call him."

Saffron wandered down the long hallway, her feet tapping

on the intricate geometric pattern of the parquet flooring, as she listened to the ringing on the other end of the phone.

"Hello?" the voice was Zayne's, but it sounded hushed and hurried.

"Zayne? This is Saffron."

"Saffron?" he seemed genuinely at a loss for a second, then must have remembered who she was, because his voice was more sure the second time, "Saffron!"

"Listen, I need to talk to you about Elyse," Saffron began.

She heard him take a sharp breath, "I have to go," he said.

"No, wait! Zayne, I need to tell you something about your wife!" Saffron realized the word was slipping out and couldn't stop it.

There was erratic breathing on the other end of the phone, as if Zayne were panicking, but he didn't hang up.

"My wife?" he said.

"Right. Your wife, Elyse."

"How do you know about my wife?"

Saffron was speechless for a moment. What should she say? That the Empress had told her he was married? That she'd seen Elyse's wedding rings? That she'd noticed his jealousy toward the accountant? They all seemed like disjointed and circumstantial facts now. But he'd admitted she was his wife, so that should make it easier to make the claim.

Before Saffron could respond, he said, "Listen, I don't know if you're working with Rossi or what, but please, just leave us alone."

The line went dead. Saffron hadn't had a chance to tell him about Elyse. All she could hope was that he would understand Elyse needed him and find a way to contact her himself.

Chapter Sixteen

The hospital was nearly empty when Saffron dropped by the next morning. She knew Elyse was getting out today and, since there had still been no sign of Zayne, she wondered if Elyse would need a ride home.

She found the star sitting up on the side of her hospital bed, waiting for a nurse to discharge her. Her skin was rosy pink again, though the woman looked genuinely exhausted. Saffron had never seen bags under the star's eyes before, or smudged makeup on her temples.

Saffron was slightly worried that Elyse would be angry with her: for the Rossi photos, for having a cottage where someone could try to asphyxiate her, for not coming to visit yesterday, but Elyse held up her arms and gifted Saffron a bright smile.

"Oh, Saffron, you saved my life!"

Saffron hugged her, "I had a little help."

"But you drove me here—" Elyse glanced down at her stomach, "you drove *us* here."

Saffron smiled, "So, how about that? Another star in the making. I heard it came as a surprise to you."

Elyse's eyes were shining, "A complete surprise! I can't

believe it, actually. I guess I've just been so busy with the travel and the film, and the photographers, I just had no idea!"

"So I assume the father doesn't know either?"

"No, but I can't wait to tell Zayne, he's going to—" Elyse slapped a hand over her mouth and widened her eyes at Saffron.

"Don't worry," Saffron said, "I already figured it out, and I'm not going to say anything to anybody."

Elyse leaned forward and took Saffron's hands in hers. From this close, Saffron could easily discern a ring-line like Zayne's on Elyse's finger. Only hers was wider—the shape of the engagement ring and wedding band together.

"How did you guess?"

"I saw your rings," Saffron admitted, "And I found out Zayne was buying a house here, and he put married on the paperwork."

"You're like a detective!"

"Heh, heh," Saffron shifted, "sort of."

"Oh, it feels wonderful for *someone* to know!" Elyse said. "I'm tired of secrets. I'm tired of living in fear of someone finding out, of having to hide how I feel about him all day on the set, of hiding from the paparazzi and everyone else."

"Why didn't you want anyone to know?" Saffron had been wondering this for days, trying to think why they wouldn't just come out with it and let people know they were in a relationship.

Elyse let go of Saffron's hands, but maintained eye contact, "It's hard to explain, but we just wanted some part of our lives that we didn't have to share with the world, you know? We've both been in the spotlight since we were kids." She sighed, "We never had a birthday party that wasn't photographed, or a bike ride that didn't appear in the magazines. We didn't feel like we could give ourselves to each other because everyone else already owns us—our agents, Blum, the public—all the time.

But if we kept it secret, then when we were together as husband and wife, it was just completely us, just the two of us, something we shared with each other and nobody else. It was this amazing gift we could give each other—a chance to be just who we were, with no public face, just us."

It was a tragically beautiful description. "I almost feel bad for finding out," Saffron admitted.

Elyse waved her hand, "Oh, with the baby on the way, it is going to come to light anyway. I just want to be able to see him and tell him about the baby before the press breaks the story," she looked concerned, and Saffron noticed her gaze shifted to the door. "I don't know why he hasn't come."

Saffron squirmed, "I did try to call him."

"You did? What did he say?"

"Well, I don't think he was very happy that I knew you were married. He hung up on me before I could tell him you were here."

Elyse's face pinched into a wistful smile, "Oh, that sounds like him. He has been the strongest proponent of keeping our marriage a secret. And it's no wonder, the way Rossi hounds him." Elyse drew her gaze back to Saffron, "You know, for most people, their everyday lives are pretty private, and then, when they get married, they do it publicly, inviting people in to share that moment with them. We're just backwards, I guess."

Saffron understood it now, even supported it. That was the thing about getting to know people, she thought: if you really listened to them, it was hard to judge them too harshly. The tabloids knew that. It's why they only gave little bits and pieces of celebrities' lives, because their whole business model depended on the world judging and categorizing these people. Saffron hoped she'd never do that again.

A loud cough at the door made Saffron turn. There, in the doorway, she saw something that stopped her heart: the hospital administrator, Makani Kawai, and next to him, Keahi.

Clinging to Keahi's arm a sour-faced Evie registered shock at seeing Saffron there.

"Excuse us a moment," Makani said, "I'm just showing Doctor Kekoa around the hospital in an effort to remind him what we have to offer here in Maika'i." To Saffron's horror, Makani looked straight at her and gave her an exaggerated wink.

Evie spoke up, her grip on Keahi's arm tightening, "Oh, I think he's plenty familiar with the limitations of this little town."

Keahi himself would have looked more comfortable in the middle of a shark tank. He patted Evie's hand, "Limitations, sure, but also opportunities."

That was the wrong thing to say. She shot daggers at him from her eyes, "I don't know why you are wasting everyone's time here," she took a step back, pulling his hand with her toward the door, "we are *not* interested in returning to Maika'i. You have an incredible practice in Boston, a prestigious place in one of the finest hospitals in the world."

Elyse spoke up from where she sat on the bed, "For what it's worth, this is a very nice hospital. They've taken great care of me here."

This seemed to diffuse some of the tension in the room. After all, the patients were what this place was really about, and Evie seemed to almost recognize Elyse.

"I'm glad to hear that," Makani said, "and I'll pass your compliment on to our care team. I know they have enjoyed having you here, Ms. Avery."

At the name, Evie's eyes widened. She looked back and forth from Elyse to Saffron as if trying to figure out how an egg farmer knew one of the planet's biggest stars.

There was no more to say. They turned and left the room. Keahi offered Saffron a half-hearted smile as he turned. She realized with horror that she hadn't said a single word the entire time. She hadn't stood up for Maika'i, or for the hospital. She hadn't even greeted them. She was certainly glad that she wasn't a star, and there had been no paparazzi to report on the painfully awkward encounter.

———

SAFFRON DROVE Elyse home and got her settled back into the cottage. She had bought three new CO_2 detectors and installed them in living room, the other bedroom, and the bathroom, meaning there was now one in every room of the cottage.

"Are you sure you feel safe?" she asked Elyse for the fifth time, "You are welcome to come and stay in my guest room in the bungalow if you're concerned."

"I'm not," Elyse said, "in fact, I don't know if I'll ever be concerned about anything except this baby again." She was glowing, full of contentment and excitement and impatience to see Zayne again. "How should I tell him?" she brushed her fingertips across the gorgeous bouquet on her table. Though some of the flowers were beginning to wilt, it was still magnificent.

Saffron had planned a few baby reveal parties in her event planning business, "I don't know, you could fill the room with pink and blue balloons, or we could get the bakery in town to do a special cake that says, *You're going to be a daddy*."

"Maybe," Elyse said hesitantly, "Or, maybe I could get him some flowers—you know, like baby roses and baby's breath, or something? And I could just write him a private card, about how I love him and can't wait to raise our child together, away from the cameras?"

Saffron liked this plan. It was true to the exclusive nature of Elyse and Zayne's relationship and their news.

"Yes!" Elyse, well into her thirties, squealed like a teenager with excitement, "he's going to flip out. I can't wait to tell him!" she looked around. "Do you think he'll be back tonight? From wherever he's gone?"

"I hope so," Saffron said, "doesn't he have to be there for shooting tomorrow?"

Elyse jumped up and went into the bedroom, returning with a sheaf of well-worn call sheets, "Hmmm. No," her voice fell, "he's shot all his scenes. He's not scheduled until the last day of filming—the day that we do the big finale on the beach."

Saffron nodded. It was the happy ending scene, where Elyse and Zayne reunited and the audience got the payoff it had been waiting for as the characters embraced on the beach in the morning sun. She'd overheard Blum discussing it with the assistant directors one day on set, and it sounded truly magical.

"He still hasn't returned your calls?" Saffron asked.

"Well, his mailbox is full," Elyse explained, "and my texts keep coming back undeliverable. Maybe he set his phone on privacy mode."

A light knock on the door made them both jump. Saffron stood and opened it. On the other side of the screen door was Ace Carnation.

"Hey, ladies," he said, his accent sharpening the words, "I just stopped in to see if my co-star there is okay."

Saffron kept herself planted between the two. Though Ace had been truly chivalrous and heroic in helping her get Elyse into the car, she knew what else he had been responsible for, and she didn't completely trust him.

He seemed to understand, "Listen, I don't want to intrude. Just checking to see that you're okay."

"I'm wonderful," Elyse called back.

"Any idea what happened?" Ace asked. His tone was leading. He was obviously fishing for information, for a story he could pass along to Rossi. Before Elyse could answer, Saffron closed the door in Ace's eager face.

Elyse looked surprised, "Um. That was a little rude."

It was time to tell her. She needed to know who she could —and couldn't—trust.

"Listen," Saffron moved back to the couch across from Elyse, "you should know that Ace has been feeding information to the paparazzi."

"What?" Elyse's expression went from surprised to angry. "Is that how they knew we were here?"

"Uh-huh. And how they always seem to find Zayne, no matter how carefully he conceals his whereabouts."

Another knock. Saffron stalked back to the door and pulled it open.

"You know," Ace said, "I've been thinking, I really have been a rat."

Saffron glanced at the open window. He'd heard her. There was no need to be discreet now.

Elyse stood and crossed the room to him, "You know, you're always trying to act like you're one of us, and I think we've treated you like that, but you must not be, if you're willing to sic the press on us."

"Listen, it's not personal. They would have found us anyway, and if I could make a few bucks, maybe it would fill the gap between our salaries a little, you know?"

The open disbelief on the two women's faces must have revealed his misstep.

"Okay, maybe that's not a great reason."

Saffron locked Ace in her gaze, "You know," Saffron said, "for someone who wants to be a writer, you're not very observant."

"Hey, what's that supposed to mean."

"It means that if you really do want to make it as a writer —and I don't mean make it as a transcriptionist, who just writes down what other people have already said—you need to look around. Find the truths in the world and write them. You and Rossi have it all wrong. You think that if you write a story, you make a truth. That's backwards. Stories don't make truths. Truths make stories."

Ace looked at her for a long time before he spoke. When he did, there was something new in his tone: an acceptance, an acknowledgement, "That's pretty good advice," he said.

———

LATE THAT AFTERNOON the storm moved out. As it pushed away, the sky became streaky, with the last of the evening light brushed underneath the clouds like a watercolor painting.

Saffron had fetched the flowers for Elyse, the "Baby Bouquet," they were calling it, and Elyse had written the card.

But Saffron was beginning to worry about Zayne. He hadn't returned, hadn't contacted Elyse, wasn't on set or anywhere in town that she could tell.

Elyse was getting frantic, sure something terrible had happened to him. Finally, Saffron called Bradley.

"Listen," she said, "I know you have plenty of other stuff going on. But I need you to keep an eye out for Zayne Grayson."

"Okay, why?"

Saffron explained briefly, and she heard Bradley clear his voice nervously on the other end of the line.

"What is it?"

"Nothing," Bradley said, "It's just, well, with everything that's happened, having a missing person makes me a little nervous. Do you think it's possible he's been, I don't know, poisoned too?"

This was something Saffron had considered, "That's why I want you to find him," she said, "as quickly as possible."

Chapter Seventeen

"**A**ction!" Elias Blum bellowed. The rain had stopped and the mild Hawaiian sky arced above them. This scene was for Ace and Adam, Adam's final scene in the film.

Ace was telling Adam, in a comical way, to go find another life since Elyse's character was over him. Adam's character was supposed to immediately notice another girl and trot off to introduce himself, thus showing that heartbreak, in the world of the big screen, did not last.

Saffron found it an incredibly satisfying scene to watch. When she told Adam later, over the extensive lunch buffet, he nodded knowingly. "That's catharsis. One of the oldest and best known principles of drama."

"Catharsis?" Saffron had heard the word, sometime in a humanities survey course back in college, but she couldn't remember exactly what it meant.

"It's the purging of emotion by discharging it through art."

"Oookay," Saffron said slowly.

"You've had this emotional experience, and it leaves you with all these tumbling emotions," Adam said, scrunching his hands together into a ball in front of his chest, "and they're just pent up in there, and your mind doesn't really know what to do with them, and your heart doesn't really know what to do with them, and then . . ." he leaned forward eagerly, "you watch a film, or you see a painting, or maybe you act in a film or create a painting, and suddenly all those emotions," he exploded his hands and arms wide, into the air around him, "are released, and maybe you cry or maybe you laugh, but you feel better."

"Yeah," Saffron said, taking another bite of lobster, "I do feel better."

SHE WAS STILL FEELING BETTER that evening when her father and Mano showed up with more of their culinary delicacies to share.

Today they had worked on traditional luau fare: kālua pua'a and poi. They had cooked the pork in a pit, and its tenderness and rich juicy smokiness was as decadent as the lobster Saffron had enjoyed for lunch.

Saffron still found it difficult to look Mano in the eye. Every time he passed the bowl of poi or asked how the movie was going, she ended up gazing past him and giving the answer to the rooster clock on the wall.

Late in the evening, as they sat in the living room eating haupia, the coconut pudding squares that completed the meal, Mano laid a hand over hers.

"Mo'opuna," he said, "have I offended you?"

"What?" Saffron heard the apology in his voice and her chest ached with guilt, "No! Of course not, Tutu."

"Then why is it that you are avoiding me? I sense there is something between us, and I don't know how it got there or how to make it disappear."

Slate stood and worked his way into the kitchen, gathering their plates as he went. Saffron knew he was giving them time and space to talk, but she tried to catch his eye and communicate to him not to go. She didn't want to talk. Slate gave her a gentle smile and shook his head slightly. He wanted her to address this with Mano, whatever it was.

"I don't know, either," she said honestly.

"Is there hurt in your heart? Anger?"

"Yes," she said openly.

Mano absorbed that. He didn't react, simply let the truth fill the room around them. It expanded in the silence until it felt as if it were pushing against the windows and ceiling, suffocating Saffron like the carbon monoxide gas in the cottage.

Still, Mano said nothing. It was as if he was content to let them both die in the grip of this enormous, unspoken thing.

Saffron was not. She began to talk, "I am angry, and I am sad, but not at you."

"Is this about your breakup with Nik?"

"No."

"Is it something I have done? Something I haven't done? I'm an old man, Saffron, and I sometimes do the wrong thing."

It broke her heart to hear him speak like this, so humbly willing to take responsibility for something that he didn't do.

"It's not you," she said, "It's not your fault. It's something I don't want to say because I'm afraid I'll hurt you."

"Avoiding me hurts, too," he said bluntly.

Saffron watched a gecko crawl slowly across the window. "I know," she said. "I feel like that gecko," she pointed at the little brown lizard, "like I'm perching in thin air, between the chasm on one side and the chasm on the other, and I can't even see what I'm walking on."

Mano smiled, "It takes great bravery to venture into such a place. You have the courage, I'm sure, to make it across to safety." He started to rise, as if he were going to leave Saffron there, with the Big Thing unsaid. She grasped his arm.

"No, wait."

He settled back down and looked at her calmly and expectantly.

"I've known this for a while, and I didn't want to tell you. It's not really my secret, and it's not really yours, but somehow we've ended up carrying it anyway."

"That's how secrets are, mo'opuna," he said.

Saffron took both his hands. She scooted forward in her chair until their knees were almost touching. She looked directly into those weathered, kind eyes, and she said it: "Keahi is on the island."

At this, Mano blinked. She had surprised him.

"I'm sorry. I should have told you earlier, but—"

"You wanted to spend some time with him yourself?" Mano assumed, "That is understandable. Is this why you broke up with Nik?"

"No, no. Stop. I wasn't supposed to know either. I only ran into him because Echo stole his keys and brought them back to me."

At this, Mano smiled. The grin didn't quite reach his troubled eyes, but it was nice to see it, anyway.

"So I ran into him, and he told me that I couldn't say anything to you, that he didn't want you to know he was back."

She could see that this puzzled Mano.

"He was homesick, maybe?" Mano guessed, "But didn't have much time? Or didn't want to inconvenience his mother by staying at home."

"I wish that was why," Saffron said.

"What was it then? Did he tell you?

"He's getting married, Mano," it felt so good to tell him, and so awful to say the words.

"Married?" Mano's eyebrows drew together and his mouth bunched, "What do you mean?"

"I mean that the reason he is here is that Evie is with him. They're getting married, but she wants to decide where without any 'interference' from his family."

Saffron had rarely seen Mano angry, but she was seeing it now. Still, he demonstrated amazing restraint. He closed his eyes and breathed for a moment. Saffron let go of his hands, and he stretched them up and out to the side while breathing meditatively. Maybe he'd been reading *Yoga for Seniors* with Slate.

When he opened his eyes, Mano looked at her, "What, exactly, did he say?"

"He said Evie wants to get married."

"Did he seem excited?"

"Not particularly. I think, honestly, that he felt bad for lying to you."

"As well he should. Saffron, the only times that my grandson and I have been at odds were times that he was walking down a bad path in his life. I think this is such a path."

"I think you may be right," Saffron was aware that she might be biased.

"But we don't know what lies along this path," Mano said, "like the little gecko walking on glass, we might not be able to see what Keahi is walking on, or where it will lead him. Let's give him some time and see what crossroads might crop up along his path, eh?"

Where Mano got his wisdom, Saffron didn't know. She assumed it was from his life experience and from the deep interconnection he had with nature. Whatever it was, it gave him insights and vision that she admired.

"There's another thing I should tell you," she said, "and it might be one of those crossroads."

He raised his bushy eyebrows.

"I may have, sort of, recommended that the Maika'i hospital ask him to come back and work there."

Mano's concerned expression transformed into a bright smile, "You see? We don't know."

Saffron thought of Evie's firm stance against the hospital, against Maika'i in general. She didn't see any reason for bright smiles. But that was what she loved about Mano. He seemed able to find a reason to smile in any circumstance.

What did bring light to her heart was that there was nothing between them now. She looked into his bright brown eyes and found herself smiling, too,

GWEN THISTLEDOWN's last scene was shot the next day. Saffron's entourage: Slate, Mano, the Empress, and the two chickens, sat at the edge of the set, watching, as she got into position under the bright lights.

She tossed them a little wave, and saw, for the first time, Elias Blum glance over to where they were sitting.

Saffron cringed. Would he yell at her? Or worse, yell at them?

When Blum bellowed, Saffron flinched. Even though she was expecting it, the volume of his voice still stunned her.

"Gwen!"

"Yes, Mr. Blum?"

"Is that your family?"

Saffron nodded.

"Why are they over there?"

"Because, I guess, they came to watch me, and nobody said it wasn't okay, and—"

"Gwen!" he stopped her, flicking a flat hand in a classic "cut" motion, "please." He looked her in the eye, "Invite them over here, under the shade. Here, by me, so they can see your performance."

Saffron felt a smile spreading across her face. She waved to her 'ohana again, this time with a "come here" gesture. They looked back, confused.

Blum untangled himself from his chair and stood, peering over the assistant directors and past the cameras to catch Slate's eye himself. He made the same motion. "Come over!" he called, "Please, make yourselves comfortable!"

Slate wheeled the Empress, and the three of them crossed the street and edged into the shade under the wide canopy where Blum sat.

"Chairs!" he commanded, and Jean Beal ran for chairs. Saffron expected folding chairs, but what she brought back were two tall director's chairs: one for Slate and one for Mano.

"I brought my own," the Empress joked. Blum kissed her hand and patted the chickens on her lap, making her giggle.

"Gwen has been a real asset to our production," he said, "you should be proud."

"We are," Slate said, settling into the director's chair, "very."

Gwen's last job in the film was to offer Elyse one last piece of relationship advice. Saffron had seen the script, the colored pages that meant Ace had changed her lines. When she'd read them, she'd been unsure exactly how they would sound when she delivered them.

But now, standing across from Elyse, with the bright lights washing out the shadows and the cameras rolling, Saffron knew exactly how to deliver Ace's words. She knew how because he had finally made a real observation. She knew because within those words was truth.

"I don't know what your future holds. Nobody does," Gwen's line came easy to Saffron, and she looked Elyse in the eye as she spoke, "but I know it can be full of magic." She reached into her voluminous shopping bag and pulled out a souvenir pen in the shape of Hawaii. Pressing it into Elyse's hand, Saffron spoke as Gwen for the last time, "Sometimes you just have to write your own happy ending."

Chapter Eighteen

I t was after that triumphant scene that Blum's underlings broke the news about Zayne.

"Disappeared?" Blum asked, "You mean took off?"

"We don't know what we mean," Jean Beal, the PA standing next to the assistant directors, said timidly. "He's just nowhere. I can't find him, can't get ahold of his cell phone, the local law enforcement hasn't seen him, or the local hospitals. No airlines have record of him traveling off the island. As far as we can tell, Zayne Grayson has just completely disappeared."

Blum dropped his head.

"We shoot the final scene tomorrow," he mumbled.

"I know, sir."

"It's the culminating scene."

"I know, sir."

"Can we get a stand-in? A body double?" one of the ADs offered.

Blum looked at him derisively.

"We need dialogue, reaction shots, *face* shots. The audience wants to see Zayne and Elyse, not Elyse and the back of Zayne's head. Nobody else can do this."

"Too bad Zayne doesn't have a twin," the other AD said.

"Too bad we didn't shoot this scene days ago," Blum said, "if not for the rain, we would have been done." if he seemed high-strung before, Blum was practically humming with nervous energy now. His face was tight, his long arms wrapped around the chair so firmly that his hands were white.

"Maybe he'll show up before his call time tomorrow?" Saffron offered.

Blum looked over at her, "Trying to lead us to the happy ending Gwen?" He attempted a smile. "Maybe. But if not, you get the writers on this. We need a new ending. A solo ending for Elyse. We may have just gone from making a romantic comedy to a dramady."

SAFFRON HADN'T YET MADE it home when her phone rang on the seat beside her.

"Answer," she said, and the phone picked up.

A deep, smooth voice greeted her from the other end of the line, "Hi Saffron, it's Morgan."

It took her a moment to place the name, "Oh, Doc Morgan! Hi! How's Echo?"

In the background, Saffron heard, "Get out of here!" The voice made her smile—Echo sounded much stronger.

"She's doing much better, thanks to your quick diagnosis!"

"I'm so glad to hear that."

"We seem to have been able to flush out the lead, and she's back on her feet."

"That's excellent. I'm glad you're here in town."

"Listen, Saffron, I wanted to call and thank you for your help with Echo, and I also wanted to ask you something else."

Saffron's heart skipped a little, "Okay."

"I'm just wondering," Doc Morgan began. Saffron didn't know what she was going to say. Was she ready to go on a date with someone new, so soon after breaking up with Nik? But Nik himself had said he wanted her to go out, to spend time with great guys. Doc Morgan seemed pretty great, though Saffron suddenly realized she wasn't exactly sure if Morgan was his first name or his last name.

And now he was waiting for an answer to a question he had asked while all that was running through her head. She had no idea how to respond.

"I'm sorry, could you . . . what was that again?" she asked.

"I was just wondering if you knew any more about the night Echo was poisoned?"

Saffron's response died on her lips. That was not the question she'd thought he was going to ask.

"A—" she stumbled, "a little."

"Okay, so it may not be important, but I'm a little worried about Echo. She's usually such a talkative bird, and now all I can get her to say are the same two sentences."

"Get out of here?" Saffron asked.

"Yep, and 'What are you doing?'"

Saffron remembered Echo asking her that on the morning she found Shar.

"Now that you mention it," she said, "that's all I've heard her say since that night. Usually, she calls me by name, demands treats, and echoes whatever anyone else says."

Something clicked in Saffron's mind. *Echoes whatever anyone else says.*

"Doc," she said, "keep her safe. I'm going to have to call you back."

Officer Bradley was weary, but willing to visit Doc Morgan's office with Saffron later that night. She was carrying the makeup kit from Elyse's cottage—the only one she could get her hands on quickly enough.

Inside the trendy, well-decorated office, Echo flapped to Saffron's shoulder and caressed her cheek. "Get out of here!" she screamed into Saffron's ear.

Doc Morgan's office had no desk. It had a couch and two chairs, a big-screen TV, and a picture window. Saffron sat on the comfy white couch and turned her head to look Echo in the eye. The bird cooed a welcome.

"So you think," Bradley said, and Saffron explained again for the third time:

"I think Echo saw something, or at least heard something. I think she has some trauma. I think she was listening when Shar was killed, and she may know something about what happened."

"So now I'm interviewing a parrot?" Bradley sighed, "Oh, Arlene Winn's going to love this. Not to mention the Honolulu boys. They already make fun of country policing." He gave Saffron a pointed look, "I filed the paperwork today. I think we've got you cleared, but I'm not sure Arlene wants to let it go, so we really need to figure this out. Soon."

"I think Echo's going to help us do that, aren't you, Echo?"

"What are you doing?" Echo screeched.

Saffron laid out the makeup kit on the couch beside her.

"I'm hoping this will take her back to that night," she said, "like a prop to set the scene." Carefully, she extricated Echo from her shoulder and set the big bird on the far arm of the couch before walking over and gesturing the men out of the room. Echo paced nervously as she watched them leave.

Closing the door behind them, Saffron stood and counted silently to ten. Bradley watched skeptically, while Doc Morgan wore an expression of amused curiosity.

After the count of ten, Saffron threw the door open, bursting into the room.

Echo raised herself up to her full height and stood stock still for a moment before screaming, "What are you doing?"

Saffron stayed still, holding a hand back to keep Bradley and Doc Morgan frozen, as well.

When Echo spoke again, her voice was different. Not Shar's squeaky mouse voice, rather an unsteady, falsely low one, "Excuse me, excuse me!"

Shar's voice again, "You're not supposed to be in here!"

The low voice, "I was just getting something for Miss Avery." Echo repeated the name twice more, "Miss Avery Miss Avery."

Shar's mouse-voice, "If she needs anything, she needs to come to us. Hey, you're the one who has been stealing stuff from our cupboards, and moving stuff around. I've been yelling at my assistant for that."

"Sorry, I'll be sure to ask next time."

It seemed like that may be the end of the conversation. Saffron was disappointed. There was really nothing in that exchange to indicate a crime.

Just as Saffron was about to approach Echo, Shar squeaked again. "Hey, wait a minute, come back here, turn around."

There was a long pause while Echo cocked her head sideways, pinning Saffron with one glassy eye.

"I said, turn around. What do you have there? More of that new blush I found in here the other day? Are you the one who left it? The one with Elyse Avery's name on it?"

"I left it for you to use on Miss Avery, yes," the other voice replied, "It complements her skin tone."

"I'LL decide what complements whose skin tone. I'm the makeup artist. Joke's on you, anyway. I took it. I think it complements MY skin tone. I hope it was expensive. Leave me the rest you have there in that bottle, if you like. It certainly won't complement YOUR skin tone."

"This bottle?" the low voice seemed more ominous with every word, especially when growled through Echo's ebony beak.

"That's not all you have there, is it? What's going on here?" Echo had Shar's voice down. The pitch, the intonation, it was as if the dead woman were speaking from beyond the grave, "Put that spirit gum down! That's not yours. You can't steal from my kit! Get out of here!"

At this, the parrot exploded, descending on the open makeup kit and raking it with her talons, flapping and spewing the various colored powders into the air and across the white leather couch. She leaped into the air, trailing powder, and flew in tight circles around the office, making the most horrific choking sounds Saffron had ever heard until she dropped from the air and landed face first on the rug, where she lay in convulsions.

The three of them rushed toward her as she churned. Even Doc Morgan was afraid to touch her. When Saffron moved toward her, he stopped her. "No, you could hurt her by restraining her, or she could use that beak and take off one of your fingers."

After a few very long seconds, Echo lay perfectly still in the center of the carpet. Around her, a rainbow halo of smudged powders that blended with the colors of her feathers and made it look as if she had melted into the white rug.

Doc Morgan stepped carefully forward. At his approach, Echo leaped to her feet, stretched her wings, and spoke.

"Saffron! Saffron!" Echo launched into the air.

"I'm right here, Echo," Saffron braced for the impact of Echo's landing.

"Wow," Doc Morgan was shaking his head, "this acting thing has gone to Echo."

"What do you mean?" Bradley was obviously still shaken by the whole spectacle.

"That right there," Doc Morgan said, "was one heck of a performance."

Saffron ran two fingers down the bird's back, "She wasn't having a seizure?"

"Nope. She wouldn't have recovered so quickly."

"She was acting?" Bradley asked.

"Acting out what she'd seen," Saffron corrected, "It was catharsis—she was discharging all that terror she'd felt and seen." It was just as Adam had described.

"Well, I'm not sure any of that is admissible," Bradley said, "but it was pretty fascinating."

"It may not be admissible," Saffron said, "but it was informative. We now know the killer's motive—Shar had seen him stealing from the makeup trailer, and she'd identified that he'd been trying to poison Elyse, and he didn't want her telling anyone."

"We think it's a 'he,' then?" Bradley clarified.

"Echo dropped her voice down when she was speaking as the killer," Doc Morgan pointed out.

"Right."

"And he was planting the poison and . . ." Bradley rubbed his temples, "stealing Spirit gum, too?"

"That's what it sounded like," Doc Morgan said.

"What in the world is spirit gum?"

Of that Saffron was unsure. She had seen the little bottles of it in the trailer, but she didn't actually know what it did.

"I don't know," she said, "but I'm sure Roman does."

"Roman? Isn't he one of our suspects?"

"Not anymore," Saffron said, "Shar talked about her assistant. She wouldn't have said that to Roman himself."

"Good catch," Doc Morgan winked. Saffron's heart fluttered a little. She was certain his wink would have that effect on anyone.

She pulled her thoughts back to the task at hand, "I'll find out what spirit gum is. But I don't think the killer got away with it, because there were some bottles of it on the floor in the trailer."

"Do you think he'll come back for it?"

"Depends on how badly he needs it."

Bradley was pacing, rubbing a boot across the smudges of powder on the rug, "It also sounds like the killer was trying to put more powder in the kit, for Elyse Avery?"

"That's right," Saffron said, "he brought a bottle of it."

"Which he must have thrown in Shar's face."

"And closed the trailer door so it stayed in there all night," Saffron added.

"Which is why it affected Echo, too," Doc Morgan reached out and stroked the bird.

They were all quiet for a long moment, the terrible thing hanging in the air around them like the makeup dust.

"Free bird!" Echo cried, and launched into another wheeling circle around the room. This time, her dips and arcs were full of jubilation.

WHEN SAFFRON CALLED HIM LATER, Roman was, as always, impatient, "Spirit gum is an adhesive. It sticks things to the skin."

"What kinds of things?"

"Scars, fake wounds, facial hair, whatever you need to stick."

"And how do you remove it?"

"It can be tricky. The best way is to use a special spirit gum remover."

"Which you keep in the makeup trailer?" Saffron said.

"Yes. There's plenty in there. The police finally let me back in, and I found three bottles of it on the floor."

Saffron thanked him and hung up. She stood and paced. Was the killer still nearby? Did he still want the remover? If so, could she think of a way to use that to lure him?

She called Bradley, "I think we should unlock the makeup trailer tomorrow. Make sure everyone on the set knows it's open now."

Chapter Nineteen

The last day of filming had been postponed. The hope was that either Zayne would return, or the writers would come up with another ending that could work in place of the joyous union of the two main characters.

Saffron was using the day to get caught up on the farm, and she was using her chores to keep from going crazy with worry about Zayne. Was he guilty, so he had fled? Or was he, himself, in danger from the killer?

"I'm sorry, girls," Saffron apologized to the hens, "it's been a crazy few days. Don't worry, I'll give you all my attention next week."

She dipped a hand into the glass jar of scratch grains on the table in the work area and walked down the aisle, tossing some into each pen. The hens converged on it, gobbling up every grain. Saffron walked along, plucking the eggs from the conveyer: an olive one, a sage one, two khakis, and a pale greenish gray that she would have called lovat. She wished Holly were here so she could show her the difference. When she turned to walk back to the front of the egg house, she saw Elyse crossing the path outside.

"Any word yet?" she called.

Elyse whirled, startled, "No, no, I haven't heard anything."

"Come in and see the hens," Saffron said, thinking that the chickens might be a good distraction for Elyse.

Her new friend was tentative as she entered. Maybe she was a little afraid of chickens, Saffron thought.

"Here," Saffron nodded toward the glass jar, "toss these to them."

For one long moment, Elyse looked from Saffron's eyes to the hens, then plunged her hand into the glass jar and retrieved a streaming handful of grains. Saffron stood very still.

Elyse's eyes. They were wrong. She'd become familiar with their clear sage green. Now, they were lovat, just like the egg in her hand.

"I just need to put these eggs in the cartons," Saffron said, "thanks for your help."

Saffron watched the star as she walked the long aisle. She was looking ragged—her hair disheveled, her eyebrows mussed and smudged. Saffron wondered again if it was caused by some kind of substance in her system. The woman had certainly had a difficult time lately.

It must be so difficult to not know where your husband was,

what had happened to him, or who was responsible. She hoped the chickens would calm Elyse.

Saffron put the eggs in the cartons one by one. Something tugged at the edge of her mind.

"Elyse?" she asked, causing the star to turn toward her, "are you doing okay? Are you comfortable in the cottage?"

"Oh, yes," the woman said, "yes, very comfortable."

Saffron looked at her closely, "Do you need anything? Fresh towels?"

"My, my make up kit?" the star asked, "I can't seem to find it."

"Oh, I'm sorry! The police took it to analyze," Saffron hoped the lie sounded convincing. It would be more complicated to tell the woman that she had borrowed the kit and a parrot had then destroyed it. Saffron leaned forward and spoke carefully, "but I think they're all done in the makeup trailer, so maybe you could get some of the stuff from there, if you want."

The actress perked up, "that would be wonderful. It's just hard to feel like me, you know?"

"Sure. I wish you could get it tonight, but there's a big crew dinner at the Oceanside Cafe and nobody is going to be around the set. Maybe you could get it tomorrow when you go down?"

The star nodded and tossed the last of the scratch grains to the hens, then made an excuse and left the egg house. Saffron watched her go with a deep feeling of apprehension.

Carrying the cartons toward the house, Saffron kept an eye on the Coral Cottage.

Inside, she stuck the eggs in her inside fridge and walked, with a knot in her stomach to the living room, where the celebrity magazines were spread across the floor and the futon.

She reached for her laptop, and for the first time in her life, began to stalk a celebrity.

Saffron wanted to know everything she could about Elyse. Had she ever been arrested? Gone to another country? She felt that hunger that some people felt about all celebrities, all the time—that craving to know everything about them. She went to an electronic encyclopedia site and searched for Elyse Avery.

It was roughly the same information she'd seen before. Elyse's early years had been full of turmoil, her parents splitting when she was two, then the children going into foster care when she was three. She'd landed with the Averys at four.

She'd had a star's childhood—growing up on studio lots, with tutors for teachers and co-stars for friends. Her adolescence had been unremarkable, except for a few rebellious parties at her parents' Beverly Hills mansion.

One interesting note was that a few years ago, in her twenties, the actress had taken online courses and gotten a bachelor's degree in accounting. That was, perhaps, where she had met Kirk Marshall.

She had acted in her first romantic comedy leading role opposite Zayne almost eight years ago, and they'd been in five films together, counting this one, since then. Saffron liked knowing that the chemistry they'd had on screen, the fireworks that all the reviews mentioned, were real.

It was growing dark when Saffron came across the single article that changed everything.

———

———

SAFFRON WAS in the middle of town, but she felt completely alone. The trailer was dark and quiet. She realized that she was unused to sitting in the dark. Generally, if she was awake, she switched on a light.

She hoped she was right about this, and then, immediately, hoped she was not. She didn't know how she possibly could be.

When the door opened, and the weak light from the street lamps along Holoholo street fell into the room, Saffron scrunched back against Echo's empty cage. The door closed behind a silhouetted figure, and Saffron tried not to breathe.

It wasn't until the figure stepped to the counter and snapped on the lights that she looked in the mirror and saw Saffron.

"Oh, Saffron!" she turned around, laying a hand over her heart, "you scared me to death."

Saffron didn't say anything.

"What are you doing here in the dark?"

"I might ask you the same question," Saffron said.

"Oh, no, I'm just here to borrow some makeup, like you suggested!" she reached for Roman's kit on the counter and started rubbing moisturizer into her skin.

"Right. I did suggest that. You might need something else from here, too, though, huh? Like some spirit gum, or spirit gum remover?" Saffron eyed the smudged eyebrows. She could see, now, something stuck in them. There was some around the woman's jawline, too.

Her laugh was high and nervous, "Well, you never know, I guess."

"I would think you would know exactly what you needed for your disguise by now, Everly." Saffron stressed the last word.

"I'm beginning to worry about you, Saffron," the woman said, fiddling with the cap on the moisturizer, "you've forgotten my name."

"No, I've just learned it." Saffron looked directly into those lovat-green eyes, "Everly. Elyse Avery's twin sister. Separated when you went into foster care at three years old. You were adopted first, but not into such posh circumstances as your sister would be six months later."

Everly's face was tight, but she didn't flinch at the truth and she didn't stop. She took a brush and started applying eye shadow.

"How did you find this out? Are you some kind of a detective?"

"Sort of," Saffron said, echoing her conversation with Elyse. They really were very similar in some ways.

"So what tipped you off?"

"Several things. For one, I found an article that mentioned Elyse's twin sister."

"You don't know how it was to grow up looking exactly like America's sweetheart, but having absolutely nothing. She wore the finest clothes, I didn't even have shoes that fit. She had a swimming pool, I didn't even have running water."

"That must have been hard," Saffron admitted.

"More than hard! People were always comparing me to her."

"The resemblance is almost perfect," Saffron said.

"Almost? It is perfect. We're absolutely identical. No distinguishing beauty marks, no scars."

"Just your eyes," Saffron said.

"What are you talking about? We both have green eyes."

"Yes, but they're slightly different shades of green."

"No they aren't."

"We'll agree to disagree," Saffron said.

"So that's what you're doing here? Trying to reveal me?"

"No, just trying to figure out why you've gone to all the trouble of dressing up like an accountant for all these years."

Everly scoffed, "That seems obvious. Nobody could know that I was here."

"Why not?"

"I figured out that we were twins in my teens. Nobody could look this alike and not be blood related. So I went to one of her parties. She was a poor little rich girl, desperate for some time to herself, a break from her perfect life. So I started standing in for her sometimes—boring parties, important tests, she slipped me some money and I showed up, put on her clothes, and she got out of whatever she wanted."

Saffron was beginning to see, "And it continued?"

"All these years," Everly said.

"Two sisters, one life."

"Nobody missed me in my own life. I might as well step into hers. And you need two people to live one celebrity life. It's intense."

"And Kirk?"

"A fabrication that made it easy to stay nearby, at least until Zayne started hanging around."

Zayne. Saffron felt her blood run cold. The one person who could ruin the charade.

"Does Zayne know?"

"Do you think he would hate Kirk so much if he did?"

"Everly, where is Zayne?"

"My husband is waiting for me in an undisclosed location."

"He's not your husband."

"That's what Elyse kept telling me. All these years of sharing a life, and this she refused to share."

"And you're done sharing a life, aren't you?"

"That's right. I'm stepping in to the role for good."

"Which is why you tried to kill Elyse, and had been trying for a while?"

Everly sighed, "It didn't have to get so . . . dramatic. If the makeup lady had just used the blush like I'd suggested, Elyse would have slowly become ill. I would have stepped in more and more, it would have been a very natural progression."

"There's nothing natural about that," Saffron said bluntly.

"But it wouldn't have been such a big deal."

"Why didn't you just put the blush in Elyse's personal makeup kit?"

"Oh, that kit isn't hers. It's mine."

That's why it was so extensive. Making herself into Kirk Marshall every day must take a lot of supplies. Even now, Everly was taking the spirit gum remover and working it into her eyebrows and along her jaw, removing the sticky spirit gum residue that had held on Kirk's eyebrows and beard.

"I will not miss this," Everly said frankly, "Fake beards itch."

"You must have a lot of experience with stage makeup. You could build a life of your own, you know," Saffron said, "Maybe you could be a makeup artist?" Saffron tried to get Everly to think of a different way forward.

"Oh, no," the imposter said, "I've been royalty. I couldn't step down to commoner."

The Hollywood hierarchy again. "You're a makeup expert, a trained accountant, but I still can't figure out how you knew about minium."

"That's easy. I grew up in Leadville, Colorado," Everly said, "We had mines there, and geology trips. Our teachers were always telling us to stay away from it. People died from it sometimes, and when I was thirteen, there was a mine collapse where several men breathed in a large amount of it and all were found dead. I remembered that. Who knew it would come in handy?"

Saffron's stomach turned. Everly was as cold as Elyse was warm, "How did you make it out to California, to meet Elyse?"

"Hitchhiked when I was seventeen."

"And you never went back home?"

"*Home* isn't the word I would use for the house I grew up in," Everly was smoothing on a creamy foundation now, freshening her look. If Saffron didn't know for sure that this wasn't Elyse, she might have been taken in, even now.

"I'm sorry that your early life wasn't what you wanted it to be."

"You don't need to be sorry. Nobody feels sorry for Elyse Avery."

"You mean Everly?"

"That's not my name. It hasn't been for a long time."

"You're not Elyse. You're not married to Zayne."

"He doesn't know that. I've had him hiding out for days, convinced that someone was trying to kill me. He'd do anything to protect me—even give up his career."

"He'd do anything to protect *Elyse*," Saffron corrected, "And how do you think he'll feel when he discovers that you tampered with the water heater and tried to kill her?"

"He's not going to find out," Everly said. She was plumping her lips with some kind of serum and smoothing on a coat of pink lipstick. Her transformation was nearly complete. She caught Saffron's eye in the mirror. "*You're* not going to tell him."

"I might."

"You won't. You won't be around to." She uncapped a big round container of loose powder and retrieved an enormous brush, which she used to pat the powder on over her finished look.

"I figured you might say that. You should know that I'm not going down as easily as Shar."

"You should know that I have other options besides lead powder. I just used that because I had it on hand."

"What about Elyse? She's alive, you know."

"She'll be joining you before the night's out. Elyse is weak. I have no doubt that I can take care of her. I'll just have to take a more direct route."

Saffron looked at her. "Zayne will figure it out, you know. You are nothing like Elyse."

"I'm confident that he won't," Everly said.

"How can you be so sure?"

"Because reality is a funny thing. You've been in the movies now. You can see how a very convincing set looks like a real town. You may know it's a set, or that it's altered, but you're willing to accept on some level that it's the real place that these real people live. You'll accept an *alternate* reality if it allows you to keep believing in the story. Zayne has a story he believes in. In it, he's the happy husband of the world's most beautiful star. He's got the wedding rings in his pocket right now, and when I get back to him, after all of you have been cleared out of our way, he's going to slip those rings on my finger. I'll keep him believing in that story, even if it's a little altered."

"And you don't have any remorse? About killing Shar? Or killing me? Or killing your own sister?"

"Why should I? Remorse is a useless emotion. It makes you do things that are not in your own best interest," Everly shrugged, "I guess it's like love that way. Yes, I killed Shar, but that kept me from being exposed, so it was a worthwhile action. The same will be true of you and Elyse. It's just the way life is."

"That's a wrap!" Saffron said loudly.

Everly looked at her, cocking her head to the side, "What?"

"I said, 'That's a wrap.' It's what you say when you get all you need out of a scene."

"A scene?"

Saffron reached under Echo's cage and pulled out the recording device she'd gotten from Rossi. At the same moment, Bradley walked in, gun drawn. He was backed by three Honolulu officers.

Saffron stood in the parking lot of Bradley's office holding Everly's phone. She dialed Zayne.

He answered, his voice panicked, "Elyse? Where are you? It's so late. I was afraid you were hurt."

"Zayne," Saffron said, "Don't hang up. I have something very important to tell you."

Saffron spent the next several minutes explaining the weird reality Zayne had fallen into. She didn't mention the baby, but she told him everything else she knew, about the twins switching in and out of Elyse's life, about Everly murdering the makeup artist and trying to kill Elyse, about Everly's plan to manipulate him into a life with her. She'd even swapped phones with Elyse to make it appear the real Elyse was calling from this number.

When she finished the line was so quiet that she was afraid Zayne had hung up.

"Are you still there?"

"Yes," he said, his voice tired, "but not for long."

"What does that mean?"

"I'm finished," Zayne said, "done. This is the last straw. I won't be manipulated anymore. Not by the press, not by my agent, certainly not by a woman who married me while she kept her twin sister a secret."

"Wait—" this was not going how Saffron thought it would.

"No. I won't be coming back to the set, and I won't be coming back to Elyse."

"What am I supposed to tell her?" Saffron begged.

"Tell her," he began, then stopped, "tell her that we never should have tried to be together. We live lies onscreen, we live lies offscreen, I guess, for us, there can never be anything truly real."

Chapter Twenty

It was the last day of filming.

Ace had stayed up all night making changes to the script. Saffron watched as he handed it to Blum.

Blum read through it, making a note here or a comment there. Finally, he looked up. "This is by far the best thing you've every brought me."

"This was supposed to be the joyful resolution," Blum said, "and for that, the morning beach scene might have worked fine. But we've rewritten it to be the poignant goodbye, and for that we need the golden hour—that late afternoon light—and a rougher terrain. We're moving the set to the lava point just outside of town."

Saffron knew that point. It was rough, dark, a sharp contrast to the smooth sky above it. The sea there was angry, with waves constantly breaking on the point and spewing seafoam and water twenty feet into the air. It seemed right for the sad turn of events in Elyse's life.

Blum walked away without waiting for discussion. From that moment on, it was all-hands on deck—the roadies moving the trailers and vans, Roman rushing around getting everyone's makeup done, the costumers putting in a tuck here and a stitch there, the lighting crew fine-tuning their equipment. Everything moved out to the lava point.

Once everything was set up, there was an undeniable energy on set, and a terrible tension that the new ending had brought.

Saffron walked along the edge of the narrow road where the trailers and vans were crammed in.

"I don't know if it will work at all," Blum was saying to his assistant directors, "We've gone from a rom-com to a dramady. I don't know if we can pull that off with all the best editing in the world, but we're going to try. I need a new title, new soundtrack, the works." Saffron stopped listening and continued down the little road to Elyse's trailer.

Elyse didn't look perfectly rested anymore. She didn't look glowing, and she didn't look bright. Saffron realized that this scene may very well be the toughest of her career.

The "Baby Bouquet" was wilting on the countertop, its card sticking up hopefully even as the roses sunk down around it. Elyse was holding her phone in her hand and she tapped the call button reflexively. Saffron waited politely as the phone rang.

"This is Zayne, leave me a message." A beep. Another recorded message, "This mailbox is full. Please try your call again later."

"I just keep trying, but he won't answer," Elyse looked at Saffron with pleading eyes. "I never meant to deceive *him*. I just —I just needed a break. I had to keep up with the sponsorships, the films. I had no idea that Everly would try to—" she stopped talking.

"Would try to steal your life?"

"I know," Elyse stood and walked around the trailer, dialing the phone again, "I should have seen it coming." Elyse looked back down at her phone, then tossed it onto the granite countertop with a clatter.

Saffron left the trailer expecting the sky to darken and rain to pour again. This was not the happy ending Gwen had promised the couple.

A shutter clicked, and Saffron turned to see Rossi duck back behind the end of the trailer. A short jog and a quick turn, and she was looking him in the lens.

"I'm sorry," he apologized, "I'm trying to legitimize, but I don't know how to use my skills to do that."

She looked at the little man, a thought dawning in her mind, "Rossi. I know exactly how to use those skills. I need you to find Zayne Grayson."

He held up his hands, "No, you were right. I need to do other things. I haven't been tailing him for days."

"Well, I want you to tail him now," Saffron said. "There's nobody who knows better where he would be. I need you to find him. Wait here," she dashed back into the trailer, and Elyse barely looked up as Saffron snatched the card from the Baby Bouquet.

Outside again, she handed it to Rossi. "And when you track him down, give him this."

———

SAFFRON HAD EXPECTED the lava point to be difficult for Elyse to climb, but she had not expected the sheer struggle that would unfold as the actress tried to make her way up the slick rocks. Whether Elyse was still weak from her stay in the hospital or whether the weight of having lost Zayne was weighing her down, she could not make it up.

The spray from the ocean spattered the silk dress, dotting it with what looked like tear stains. Saffron wanted to run to her, but the cameras were rolling.

She expected Elyse to give up, to sit down and weep in the center of the rough lava point, but the actress struggled upward, reaching the top before she crumpled to her knees amid another enormous spray of sea foam.

She was close now, and Saffron could see the pain in her sage-green eyes. She glanced at Blum. Would he stop this? Turn off the cameras? But he stayed wrapped around his chair, immovable as the waves crashed and the sun sank lower and lower over the vast ocean.

Finally, he raised a hand in readiness to cut the film. But before he finished the movement, something moved among the rocks on the other side of the point. Blum's hand froze in midair, and the cameras kept rolling as a disheveled Zayne Grayson appeared, struggling up to stand before Elyse.

Nobody on set said a thing. Blum gave no direction, yet the scene playing out between Elyse and Zayne was perfect in its pacing, in its blocking, in its raw and real emotion.

Zayne took Elyse's hands and helped her to her feet.

He paused, looking in her eyes, and knelt, offering a black velvet ring box. She nodded. Wordlessly, he pulled the rings out and slipped them into their rightful place as another spray of water danced behind them, catching the rays of the setting sun. Zayne stood. Elyse's microphone picked up his voice as they embraced.

He said, in a voice rough with emotion, only four words. They were more sincere than any script: "You are my reality."

———

THE WRAP PARTY that night was happier and brighter because of the fear they'd had hours earlier. It was at the event center, and Blum, the cast, the crew, and lots of townspeople were there.

There were two notable absences, though. The principal

actors were nowhere to be seen. In fact, only Belle Tucker at Tropical Adventures travel agency knew where they had eloped to.

Blum was relieved that his rom-com wouldn't need a new title or soundtrack and Saffron was relieved she could step out of the spotlights and back into the solace and serenity of the Hau'oli ka Moa egg farm.

Sneak Peek Book 11: Chicken Out

Saffron didn't breathe. She crouched in the dark, feeling the fabric of her costume bunching at her waist.

Tikka, her gold and black hen, wriggled and growled her displeasure. Saffron's heart raced. She put a hand over the chicken's head to calm her. Tikka could be vocal, and an outburst now would be disastrous.

The sounds of the shuffling footsteps chilled Saffron's

blood. She could see, through the crack at the bottom of the door, the wavering light growing brighter as her stalker approached. Would he know where she had hidden? Maybe he would think she'd gone on down the hall into one of the bedrooms or the big linen closet. If he passed by, she could throw open the door and run for her life—down the wide staircase, through the big entryway, out the front door, to the place where the people had gathered in a tight, secure knot to wait for help.

She saw his feet, swathed in white bandages, pass by. They paused at the far wall and turned, the light sweeping the floorboards. A roach fled the light and Saffron heard it scrabbling.

Please, she begged silently, *please, don't come this way.* If the roach raced under the door into this dark space with her, she didn't know if she could keep from screaming.

The foot, trailing a banner of pale fabric behind it, reached for the fleeing roach, and the insect veered off its course. Saffron saw its dark shape scoot directly toward her, slipping under the door.

Before she could scream, before she could leap to her feet stomping and swatting it away, Tikka's strong beak darted downward. There was a sharp tap and a wet crunch, then Tikka gave a little swallow and the bug was gone.

Saffron petted the hen's soft feathers, thinking *Thank you* very hard. Tikka may not be able to hear the expression of gratitude, but Saffron hoped the chicken could sense it.

It wasn't yet time to celebrate, though. The menacing figure beyond the door had grown still. His shuffling footsteps were silenced. He had heard the tap of Tikka's beak on the boards.

The old house smelled of dust and damp. The air in the playroom was stale. It gathered in Saffron's throat like sand. If he found her, he would kill her. Because she knew.

The cough began in her belly, and she clenched her

stomach muscles under the white padding of her costume to stop it. But it rose to her chest, her throat, the sand burning her lungs, her breath gathering like a great storm until she could no longer contain it.

The sound was sharp and rough, a cough half-swallowed, but it was enough. The wrapped feet moved again, this time directly toward her.

Join Saffron and the hens on a spooky Halloween adventure in Chicken Out: Book 11 in the Aloha Chicken Mysteries!

DEAR READER,

Thank you for visiting Maika'i and the Hau'oli ka Moa Egg Farm! I hope you enjoyed Chick Flick, and I hope you'll read more of Saffron's adventures in Book 11: Chicken Out. If you did enjoy the book, please consider writing a review on Amazon and Goodreads. I love hearing from my readers and your reviews help other readers find my novels! I truly appreciate every review and every reader who spends time with Saffron, the hens, and me!

-Josi Avari